PSYCHOTIC ESCAPING JUSTICE

MARK HAYHURST

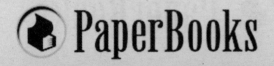

Paperbooks Ltd, 3rd Floor, Unicorn House
221-222 Shoreditch High Street, London E1 6PJ
info@legend-paperbooks.co.uk
www.paperbooks.co.uk

Contents © Mark Hayhurst 2009

British Library Cataloguing in Publication Data available.

ISBN 978-1-9065585–1–2

Set in Times
Printed by J F Print Ltd., Sparkford, Somerset.

Cover designed by:
Gudrun Jobst
www.yotedesign.com

This one's for Murphy

Acknowledgements

There are a few sick brains I picked in order to make this book nicely twisted so a big thanks to Lesley, Kaye Boy and Dr Titley

urge; Noun, a strong impulse, inner drive, or yearning; Verb, 1. to plead with or press someone to do something; 2. to advocate earnestly and persistently;3. (often foll. by on)to force or hasten onwards.

PSYCHOTIC
JULIE NEWTON

As I drive down here tonight, I need to remind myself once again that looking through people's bedroom windows is a numbers game and, sooner or later, I'm going to see some fit young bird lying spread-eagled naked on her bed, frigging herself off.

Don't get me wrong here. I'm not some avid full-time peeping tom or anything like that, I'm simply a casual, passer-by enthusiast. Not that my enthusiasm has ever yielded any noteworthy results, mind you; I've never seen anything that's any good. Oh... I tell a lie. I got a bit over-excited at seeing a massive pair of tits before I realised it was a fucking Jordan poster on someone's wall, and I saw some sixty-odd-year-old woman in a bra once. It was shit... But I knocked one out over it, anyway.

I wish she'd keep the bastard noise down back there; the banging and bashing from the car boot is doing my fucking head in. If she'd just chill out for a bit, it'll all be over. I'm letting her go free, you see; she's a lucky one. Well, if I'm honest, it's not so much her being lucky as me being a bit sloppy, really.

I had it all worked out and I slaved tirelessly to make sure there'd definitely be nothing linking me back to the rest of them. I had to choose incredibly carefully after the close shave I'd had with the first one, and the rest were planned to perfection, but this time around I've managed to let too much emotion creep back in and that's never a good idea in this game. Don't misunderstand me. It's not that my choices aren't emotive because they most certainly are; it's just that I can't really justify torturing and killing somebody that doesn't truly deserve it, and I absolutely will not have it link back to me, so I need plenty of suspects and a solid reason for my victims to deserve my special breed of justice.

This is where I messed up with this one; I knew her. Julie Newton. When I started at primary school, she used to sit next to me and for my first year of school she used to spend a large proportion of the day with her hand cupping my cock and balls. I was too young to get an erection but not so young that I didn't enjoy it. Then, in the second year, much to my disappointment, she ended up sitting somewhere else.

I didn't have much to do with her after that until a couple of years later, when it came to moving to junior school and I was put next to her again. On the first day, I was looking forward to seeing what her reaction would be when my cock started to swell in her hands, but she didn't try to touch it. Eventually, after a couple of weeks, I plucked up the courage to suggest that she gave it a grab and she looked horrified, raised her hand and grassed me up in front of the whole class. It was seriously embarrassing. That's not why she's locked in the boot, though.

When we went to high school, the classes were split up to match the intelligence level of the pupils. She was in class one (stupid) and I was in class two (a little bit less stupid). I would like to take this opportunity to point out that I was never actually stupid, school just held little interest for me. Thankfully, she wasn't so stupid, either, and our paths ended up crossing again when we were both promoted to class four in the third year.

Now, for the first two years of school all the bright kids had been learning German, so when we got moved up we were two years behind. The teacher eventually told us that it was probably for the better if we found an empty classroom and spent the double period studying.

And boy, did we study; biology mainly. By the time we'd reached the fourth year, Julie had developed into a seriously fit-looking bird. She was taller than most of the boys and had an excellent figure, great legs and to this day the best pair of soft, large, pert breasts I have ever squeezed. Her hair was blonde, her eyes were blue, her features were perfect and she had skin like that fine, almost translucent china. If someone was making a film and wanted to cast for the part of an angel, she'd have won the audition hands down.

Our shenanigans started off quite innocently in that she used to get me to play with her hair as she rested her head on the table. But, as the weeks progressed, she asked me to tickle her neck, then her back, then she'd untuck her school shirt so I could touch her skin. Every time my hand passed across her bra straps, I had to struggle not shoot a load straight into my pants.

As the weeks progressed, I got more and more confident and slowly started making my way around the front, her tight perfect stomach at first and then her breasts, over the bra. Soon I progressed to removing the bra and spending the best part of the hour just softly caressing her amazing tits. I remember how much my heart would pound as I pushed my luck a little further each time. Each time thinking that for certain she'd stop me, bollock me and call me a perv. But she never did. The first time I went underneath the bra, I could hear my heart pounding in my ears and feel the blood throbbing as it rushed to my cock.

After a few weeks of this, we had a break in the routine when Julie brought her mate's diary in and we sat and read it. I remember thinking at the time how fucking stupid girls were for keeping all this personal information in one place, and made a mental note to always try and treat them okay, even if they didn't deserve it, so that I didn't end up as a page in some crazy adolescent tome full of periods and fancyings for teachers.

On this particular occasion, the bit in her diary that had caught our attention was a part in which she mentioned being 'fingered'. Julie's friend Katy, the owner of the diary, was known as Kit Kat around the lads' changing rooms because at some time or another nearly everyone in the football team had got four fingers up her. In fact, one lad even held up his hand in what looked like a Vulcan greeting and proclaimed that he'd stuck two in the pink slot and two in the stink pot.

She didn't mention this in her diary, though. It was quite a blunt entry in all honesty; it simply said, *24th August, Jamie came around to mine when mum and dad were at bingo. Sucked tits and fingered.* Julie mentioned that this was something she had never done, so I took this as a signal that she was interested and casually offered to do it for her. I'd like to point out that I'm not nearly as cool as the word 'casual' makes me sound; my casualness was only on the outside, I was nearly having a spunk implosion on the inside. I decided to confess that I'd never done it before, either. I did this for two reasons; first, because I wanted her to feel comfortable and second, because if I did it wrong, it wouldn't be my fault. She told me to tickle her legs, to start at the bottom by her ankles and work my way up to the top. So I did.

There I was, slowly working my way up those smooth, long, pale legs, my brain doing two jobs at once; concentrating on making sure I was doing the best, delicate, soft stroking I had ever done, and concentrating on not exploding straight into my school trousers. This particular part started to get really difficult as I got to the knee, because I almost lost control when I had to start sliding her skirt up.

As I got towards the top of her legs, she slowly started to open them and once they'd completely yawned awake I began to rub her, first on the outside of her white cotton knickers and then, once I started to feel them get damp, I moved slowly to the inside. At this point she leaned over and started to kiss me. I was amazed. She was good-looking and popular and I was a nobody, yet here I was copping off with her, my hand rubbing her warm, wet, virginal vagina. She undid my trousers and grabbed my cock. She started by just squeezing it slowly for a while before she went for it and began properly pulling me off.

If there's one good thing she taught me, it was fucking cock control, and I held on as long as possible before my spunk finally projectiled across the table and splatted onto the tile floor. Looking back on it now, I could have done a much better job of the whole thing. I didn't even know what a clitoris was at that age so I just fucked her with my finger. It must have been pretty crap for her. It wasn't for me, though; I relished every single millisecond of the entire experience. Jesus! It was over sixteen years ago and I still fucking wank over it now. It was such a relief to finally blow my load. For weeks, I'd been going home with my swollen balls aching so much that I couldn't sit comfortably on the bus, rushing home and having to wank really carefully because the jiggling motion felt like being kicked in the nads. But not on that day. Oh no, that day I marched out proud, took a comfortable bus ride home, strutted back into the house, headed straight to the bathroom, threw caution out of the window and wanked the fucker for everything he was worth.

Heading into school the morning after, I still couldn't believe what had happened and I was busting to shout it from the rooftops – that's the fingering I'm on about, by the way, not the pain-free wank I had at home. So anyway, the day after, I confided the details of my dalliance with the sexy and popular Julie Newton in confidence to my mate Andrew and the cunt only went up and asked her, to see if I was bullshitting. She was horrified that I'd betrayed her trust, but rather than just deny it, she made it worse. She told him it did happen and that I had a tiny penis. Which I don't have, by the way.

So for the rest of school I was cursed with a nickname that to this day is still used if I bump into an old classmate. My name is Jeremy Wilkinson, but I used to get called Will for short; after this incident I was 'Two Mil Will'.

*

The following two years were horrible and that's why I wanted to get my revenge on her. I wanted to beat her, then tie her up, then show her just what my 'two mil will' was capable of.

Emotion had crept in and damned nearly ruined everything. It's like being on the school bus with aching bollocks all over again. She's there in the boot, half naked, gagged and bound, and I could have her whenever I want, but that would leave a trace. It's a fucking shame. That was my first rule; don't have sex with them, no matter how much you want to.

So I'm going to just drop her off in the middle of nowhere. I've been careful; I'm pretty sure she's not seen me and she doesn't know where she's been, where she's going, or what sort of car she's in. She's too out of her face for that, although I'm fairly certain she does know this car has a spacious boot. I hope she appreciates it.

It's probably partly her fault that I became fixated with sex. God only knows how differently I would have turned out if I hadn't had my cock and balls fondled for the best part of a year when I was four years old, although at least when she did it, I liked it, not like when that fucking bastard did it.

I'm impressed with how I caught her, though. It was great. I'd seen an article in the *Gazette* about sloppy police work and potential corruption within the local force and noticed her name below it. I didn't even know it was definitely her as she was certainly old enough to have got married and it's not the most unusual name, but Holme Bridge isn't a big place and I was damn sure going to fucking find out. I called her, pretending to be a police officer and her voice sounded familiar, which gave me a bit of confidence. I told her I had some very important information that should be put into the public domain and I arranged to meet her in the car park of the Nobody Inn, a pub that's been closed for about two years now. I told her I was choosing there so that I wouldn't be seen, and insisted on anonymity.

I was actually choosing that location because I can see it easily from my attic room. The pub's just a ruin now, it was always doomed. Some freak was looking after it who died in a car crash, which I narrowly avoided by the way. Then, once it reopened, it wasn't long before another car came speeding around the corner and this time it actually hit the building. It was a tragic but fucking funny accident. It was a husband and wife and she'd been sucking him off while he was driving. He must have lost concentration and as he rounded the corner, he smashed the car into the side of the pub. When the fire brigade removed the wreckage, they found them both dead. In the impact of the smash, as the front of the car buckled, the steering wheel had jammed the woman's head in her bloke's crotch and forced her mouth closed. She was removed with his detached cock stuck down her throat.

Then last year a trucker was coming around the corner and passed out. It turned out he was diabetic and driving illegally, and his truck went straight into the side of the pub. He survived, as it happens, but a lot of the locals didn't, and nor did the pub.

The fire brigade failed to realise that the lorry being stuck there was the only thing holding the fucking pub up, so when they removed it, around two thirds of the building collapsed on top of everybody inside.

Due to some small print loophole, the insurers didn't pay up, so the brewery just made the remainder safe and now it sits there, boarded up, propped up with metal stilts and bouldered in. They always put boulders round everything that's derelict around here, especially abandoned car parks; it stops the gypsies getting their caravans in. Christ, not long ago they even occupied a car park that was still in use. It took ages for the police to get rid of them – it's not like they could clamp them, I suppose; that'd just ensure they stayed. They sent out a gypsy liaison officer from the council to negotiate with them. A fucking gypsy liaison officer! I never even knew such a thing existed. Now they've cleared off, but some smart arse has meddled with the tariff sign so that it reads: *One hour – sixty pence. Two hours – a pound. Gypsies – free for a week.*

I digress; back to the point. I've been experimenting with different types of poison and venoms over the last six years and I've built up quite a collection of highly illegal pets and concoctions. I've had varying degrees of success over time, and I've become quite the expert now. I decided to try saxitoxin on this occasion; it's found in marine algae but sometimes finds its way into shellfish and poisons people if they eat it. It was a risky choice because I'd not tried it out on my guinea pig, and was fully aware that too much could give Julie respiratory failure and not enough would simply make her very ill. The effect I needed was temporary paralysis; I wanted her to realise what was going on, to a certain extent. Chloroform would be good if it behaved the way they lead you to believe on television, but I found out that both the dosage and results are a lot more complex than they ever seemed on *The A-Team* or *Knight*

Rider. Mind you, if it was as simple as popping a few drops on a hanky and shoving it around somebody's mouth to knock them out, it'd be pretty boring. Even if it knocked them out for long enough, you wouldn't be able to really scare them, although it does help. Something that stops the body from functioning but keeps the senses aware is much more fun. You can still do what you want, but you get the satisfaction of knowing that they're aware of what's going on and just can't do anything about it.

I knew from looking on the web that just 0.2 mils was a lethal dose for a human, so I'd carefully measured out half that, mixed it with a shot of vodka and popped it into a syringe. Most standard injections have an alcohol base, you see, and vodka is a pretty clean spirit so it works quite well. I just needed to keep my fingers crossed that she'd not put on a shitload of weight since we left school, or the effects could be compromised.

The easiest way to actually administer this particular substance is through food, but there was no guarantee I could get her back here to do that – certainly not without her seeing my face – and in this game you need to keep one step ahead all the time. I made more than my fair share of mistakes at the beginning, but I could afford to back then. Nowadays, the fucking police are all over the place like a bastard rash and I'm fully aware of just how careful I need to be.

Once I'd got the toxin sorted, I unpacked a small manual ventilator I'd had delivered a few weeks earlier and read the instructions, to make sure that if she did end up getting short of breath I'd be able to keep her alive. I couldn't believe it was so easy to use; just pop the plastic mask over her face and depress, and release the large rubber balloon attached to it. Simple. And a fucking rip-off. It cost me nearly two hundred quid.

So, I was sorted, my toxin and my safeguard were ready, now it was just a matter of timing. I'd arranged to meet her at midnight, as all the old dears who live surrounding the pub would definitely be tucked up in bed by then. I sat in my darkened attic room looking through the windows with the binoculars, waiting for her to arrive. My eyes were straining, as it was dark and I was concerned that I might not be able to see her arrive, but my fears were quashed at about five past, when I saw a pair of headlights pull on to the street before stopping by the boulders. She was driving an old Lexus. That surprised me, because I thought that the *Gazette* would pay shit money. Perhaps she was freelance, or had a boyfriend with a bit of cash or something.

As she exited the car, I zoomed in on the vehicle to make sure there wasn't anybody else in it. It was clear, so I popped on my jacket, scarf and baseball cap, carefully put my syringe and ventilator into separate pockets and set off out. I sprinted around the corner, and as soon as I had the pub in view I began to walk casually. She could see me, but I was too far away for her to be able to identify me properly even if it was daylight, as I had the cap low and the scarf high. I waved and she waved back. I'd figured that if I waved first, she wouldn't see it as a threat when I started running towards her; hopefully, she'd just assume I was getting a wriggle on because I was late. It worked a treat. I ran towards her with my head bowed slightly, but instead of slowing down as I got closer to her, I charged full pelt at her. As we fell to the floor, I got the syringe from my pocket and pumped my concoction into her thigh. She struggled for a small while, biting my hand as I tried to keep her mouth shut, but she didn't make much noise.

Then she started to convulse and I was concerned that the dosage was wrong, but after a few seconds her legs stopped kicking. The rest of her was still moving as if she had an electric current going through her, but there was definitely no resistance from the legs. After what seemed like another ten seconds or so, this had spread until just her head was shaking, pretty violently, too. I was concerned she might do herself an injury, but then, after a few seconds, it stopped. I rolled her over, took off my scarf and tied it around her eyes as I was unsure whether she'd be able to see me or not in her state. Then I went through her pockets and found her car keys. I pressed the unlock button and carried her over to it. She wasn't very heavy and I was concerned that the shot might have killed her. I didn't have time to piss about checking at this point, though, so I quickly opened the back door of the car. It was a shit-hole inside, it was obviously hers and, by the look of it, it was also her office. Papers and notes were scattered in and amongst the empty food packets and empty Volvic bottles. I picked her up and threw her on all the crap across the back seat before getting in the driving seat and carefully driving away.

I was aware that, if she knew what was going on, there would be a good chance she could narrow down a police search if I only drove around the corner, and that would have potentially caused me problems later on, so I took a drive for twenty or so minutes on the country lanes around Holme Bridge before returning home. I had to stop a couple of times to ventilate her; every now and then she'd do a dry gasp and panic would shoot through me.

Once I got to my street, I had a good look round before I risked opening my garage door. I chose this house because of its location. I'm surrounded here by small families in the main. I originally thought that living around old people up near the Nobody would be best, but they're proper nosy old cunts. They've got fuck all better to do with their time than be in everyone's business. Families are much better; they're more insular and they're too busy to notice what's going on under their noses. They also all sleep pretty heavily. Kids sleep well, anyway and the adults are fucking knackered, what with

17

working all day and looking after kids all evening. It's perfect.

Anyway, the coast was clear this night as it usually is, so I pressed the button on my keys to open the garage and carefully, quietly, reversed the Lexus in before pressing the button again to lower the door. Once inside, I got her out of the car and carried her through the internal door and into the house. I laid her carefully on the floor whilst I went back to lock the car and the door then, once I was back in the house, I opened the basement hatch and went down to check that everything was in order. The shackles were secure, the room was clean, the mattress was clean and all of the tanks and cages were in order.

I brought her down and laid her on the mattress, then carefully removed all of her outer clothing. Not for any sexual reason just yet; I just wanted to dispose of the clothes to make sure that any trace of me was wiped from them. Then I lifted her and placed her on her back on the mattress to shackle her up.

Once I'd finished, I put the clothes into a bin bag for later disposal, then I went into my bedroom and turned on the computer. I have a webcam set up down there and, as I watched her lying lifeless and limp, I wanked. It felt good to be able to do it for me this time and I came almost immediately. Unfortunately though, as soon as I had and the excitement had lifted, reality and remorse landed on me like gravity on steroids. What a fucking idiot! Everybody I went to school with knew I had a grudge against her and, unlike the rest of my victims, she'd done absolutely nothing seriously wrong. I knew I'd just have to wait a while and then dump her off somewhere. Her car posed problems of its own, but with my contacts in the trade, shifting a dodgy motor wasn't too tricky a business.

ESCAPING
THE ROOM

"Where am I? What's going on? Why am I here? What is this place?"

He's sitting up on the bed, looking around the room, and he's going to have a lot more questions before he starts getting any answers. He frowns as he vacantly glances around for a short while and then suddenly the look on his face changes as he realises he doesn't even know who he is. Considering the circumstances, he seems to take it quite well; he doesn't really panic... he just looks even more confused.

He stands up and scans the room, properly this time. It's square, with a single bed down the side of one wall and a small table down the wall opposite. There's no window and no visible source of light, but somehow the room seems to be illuminated. He can see everything very clearly. Not that there's much to see. White walls, white table, white bed, white bedding, white floor and a white ceiling, even his pyjamas are white.

He sits back down on the bed with his head in his hands and ponders again about who he might be and how he came to be here, and a few strange thoughts pass through his mind. He thinks he must be English. He deduces this because he's thinking in English.

He decides he can't just sit around all day thinking, so he

stands up and places his hands on the wall, slowly stroking it. He's looking to see if there's a concealed exit. He's extremely thorough and continues to do this patiently, the whole way around the room. First the walls, and then he stands on the table and checks the ceiling. Nothing. Then he checks the floor, slowly feeling every inch of it. He works his way from the side where the table was to the opposite one. He stands up to move the bed so he can finish his inspection and finds a pencil lying underneath it. He picks it up and looks at it. It's just a normal pencil. The black point of the lead is a stark contrast to the white in the room.

He finishes his inspection and sits on the bed. He's been in here for hours and he still has no idea what's going on. His patience is starting to wear thin. "How long have I been here?" he says, and realises he's definitely English, no question.

He concentrates hard, but there are no memories there, except of him just checking the room and finding the pencil. He lifts his arms to smell his armpits... they don't smell. He rubs his chin to feel for stubble and he's pretty clean-shaven so he decides he can't have been here very long. He wonders how many hours on different days he might waste, or have already wasted, checking the room for an exit if his memory isn't up to scratch. Then he has an idea. He smiles to himself, takes his pencil and writes on the ceiling above the bed: *You have been here at least one day*.

"There, now I'll know," he says. He begins to write again. *Don't bother checking the room for an exit. You did it yesterday, every inch from top to bottom and all you found was a pencil.*

Then he draws a small circle in the middle of the floor and puts the pencil in it, walks back to the bed, lies down and tries to get to sleep to test his theory.

After a few hours of tossing and turning, wondering how he could manage to read, write and recognise a pencil when he doesn't even know his own name, he finally drifts off to sleep. He rests soundly for hours and then he awakens.

"Where am I? What's going on? Why am I here? What is this place?"

He sits up and looks around the room, then flops back down on to the bed. He notices the writing above him. "Is this a joke? Hello! Hello! Can anyone hear me?"

He looks across the room and sees the pencil lying on the floor. He's confused. He walks over and picks it up. He's suspicious of the writing's advice.

"Did someone write that to stop me looking for an exit? Maybe there is one and they just don't want me to check!"

He begins to check the room again, just as thoroughly as the first time, in exactly the same order. Walls, ceiling, floor, and then continuing across until he needs to move the bed. He realises that the writing was correct – there's definitely no exit. He sighs, laughs at himself and then takes the pencil; he begins to write on the floor, right at the back where it meets the wall under the bed.

Told you.

He sighs again, and then looks at what he's just written and realises that it's the same handwriting as the other words he'd seen. So it must have been him who'd written them. He pushes the bed back against the wall and sits on it. He wishes there was a mirror so he could see what he looks like. Maybe he would recognise his face and remember who he is. Then he lies down on the bed, looking up at the writing on the ceiling. He picks up the pencil and changes the message, putting a neat line through the word *one* and replacing it with *two*. Then he squeezes an 's' on the end of *day* before writing in small letters, *The day before*, before the word, *yesterday*.

two
You have been here at least ~~*one*~~ *days*

Don't bother checking the room for an exit. You did it the day before yesterday, every inch from top to bottom and all you found was a pencil.

"There, that'll do"

He realises he needs to write something else so that when he wakes up again he'll know without question that it's definitely him leaving the messages. He gets up off the bed and begins to write in large block capital letters on the wall facing it.

YOU MUST HAVE LOST YOUR MEMORY BUT YOU DEFINITELY WROTE THIS. WRITE SOMETHING, THERE'S A PENCIL IN THE MIDDLE OF THE FLOOR IN THAT CIRCLE. YOU'LL SEE IT'S YOUR HANDWRITING.

He puts the pencil in the circle and walks back to the bed. He sits up to check that he can definitely read the writing from where he'll wake up. It's certainly big enough, but maybe not bold enough to catch his eye straight away. He picks the pencil back up and makes the lettering thicker, puts the pencil back and has another look. Yes, that'll do nicely. As soon as he sits up, he'll notice that without a doubt.

Eager to try out his theory, he lies down and tries to sleep. He seems to drop off a lot more quickly this time and sleeps soundly for hours before waking up again.

"Where am I? What's going on? Why am I here? What is this place?"

He sits up and reads his message.

"Write something?"

He reaches over from the bed, grabs the pencil and writes

SOMETHING

on the wall to the left of him. The writing certainly looks the same. He's really confused. He begins looking around the room and wondering where the exit might be.

He begins another thorough search and sees *Told You* written on the floor when he moves the bed.

"What does that mean?"

He puts the bed back and lies down, then notices the writing on the ceiling.

two

You have been here at least ~~one~~ days.
Don't bother checking the room for an exit. You did it
the day before yesterday, every inch from top to bottom
and all you found was a pencil.

The writing under the bed makes sense now. He walks to the back wall and underneath his big bold writing he adds:

P.S. LOOK UP!

"That should do it."

He jumps on to the bed and looks up. Then he amends the writing on the ceiling, changing the two to a three and putting another 'the day before' in even smaller writing above the previous one. Then he pauses to think for a moment and adds something extra.

~~two~~ *three*

You have been here at least ~~one~~ days
Don't bother checking the room for an exit. You did it
the day before yesterday, every inch from top to bottom
and all you found was a pencil. This isn't a good way to
keep track of time, there's a tally over there.

Tired after all his room-searching, he places the pencil in the circle on the floor, lies down on the bed and falls asleep.

"Where am I? What's going on? Why am I here? What is this place?"

He sits up and reads the bold message on the back wall.

"Write something?" he queries.

He looks at the wall to his left and something is already written there. He reaches over to the circle, picks up the pencil and then he writes something there as well; it's obvious it's the same handwriting. He looks above him as instructed, reads the message and walks over to the desk to start a tally. He draws one single line and, just to make sure there's no confusion, he adds some detail above it.

This tally started on day four!
I

Part of him wishes he'd not left himself all these notes because there's not really that much to do. At least, if he could check the room, it would kill a few hours. He paces the room back and forth, and out of sheer boredom he walks slowly from one side to the other, putting one foot exactly in front of the other like a tightrope walker. It's fifteen of his feet wide and fifteen of his feet long. He decides to write this measurement on the right hand wall so that he doesn't do it again and then, exploding from the silence, comes an almost deafening noise.

A constant beep is piercing his ears and vibrating around his head. He drops the pencil, covers his ringing ears and screams in agony. As he does this, he falls to the floor and begins to writhe around. Every bone in his body aches. Then, as suddenly as the noise came, a jolt of electricity fires through his body and a tidal wave of memories begins to wash over his once empty brain. He scrambles around on the floor for his pencil and begins to scribe on the wall. He remembers at least fifty things for every one he manages to write down, but writes as much as he can anyway. He might need this information tomorrow.

James, Nadia, Holme Bridge, Ibiza

He has to stop and cover his ears again; still screaming with pain another jolt fires through him and he begins to write once more, this time on the floor.

Crash, **Dad, Dad, DAD, DAD, DAD**

As he scribes, the nurse looks across the room at his lifeless body lying in the bed the same way it has been doing for the last four years. She sits frozen with shock, simply watching, paralysed, as the doctor struggles to revive him and screams for her assistance.

He stops writing again to hold his ears and notices a hole beginning to form in the centre of the circle which he now vividly remembers drawing with the pencil the first day he was here. The rate at which it's growing panics him and he can't think what to do. He peers down into it but sees no bottom, just a tunnel down into infinite blackness. Its spreading slows down and stops, easily wide enough for him to fit through. The sides look almost soil-like. He's spent all this time trying to figure out how to get out of this room, but now that the exit has made itself obvious, he's scared to go down.

The nurse snaps out of it and begins to comprehend what's going on. Still shocked, her chin begins to quiver and her eyes fill with water. As she blinks, a tear rolls down her cheek and splashes onto the cold tile floor, then she rushes across the room and begs with the doctor to try again.

He removes the covers from the bed and begins to tie them together to form a rope. Concerned that it won't be long enough, he removes all of his clothing and ties them together, too. He positions the bed over the hole and ties one end of his rope to the underside and the other end around his waist.

He sits down on the floor and pushes his feet under the bed and into the hole. He turns his body around and, resting on his stomach, he pushes out his legs to brace them against the soil wall's side in an attempt to control his descent. He slowly lowers himself into the tunnel and, as he lowers himself, he pushes out his arms to brace himself further. Balanced across the tunnel, his body outstretched like a human star, he worries if he'll be actually able to descend safely and, if not, whether the makeshift rope will hold. Then carefully, moving one arm or leg at a time whilst bracing himself with the others, he lowers himself further and further into the hole. He carries on for quite some way and then, once again balanced with legs and arms outstretched, he peers down into the darkness and sees nothing.

The noise stops as suddenly as it had started and the shock and relief of it causes him to fall into the darkness. The drop seems never-ending and as he falls, gaining more and more speed, the sheet around his waist pulls tight as the slack disappears, and then snaps. Amidst the fear, one thing is buzzing around his brain, the last word he wrote.

DAD

JUSTICE
JULIE NEWTON

Well... What a right old mess all this is turning out to be. I don't even know where to start; just as I thought we were about getting somewhere with tying a few things together, that silly cow from the *Gazette* prints an extremely dubious story and everything's all thrown into turmoil.

Then, as if the atmosphere around here wasn't bad enough, she went missing in what could only be described as 'convenient' circumstances. The Chief had already had to suspend my mentor, Detective Inspector Tim Morris, because he was implicated in the newspaper story and Julie Newton's disappearance has just made it worse for him. It seemed a little convenient that she should disappear in exactly the same no-trace way as a few other people we were working on linking...

I became involved in a few murder cases as part of my training. Not so much to solve them, I'm far too junior for that, but for research and what have you. It was whilst looking over some of the local cases that I noticed a few of them seemed to have similarities that had been overlooked by head office. I only came here from uniform six months ago and was asked to shadow Tim as part of my career development, but in and amongst dealing with the more boring stuff, and in my own time, I've been working on the potential link between a few murders around the Yorkshire area. Unfortunately though, since everything kicked off around here I'm now the only person left in the local CID office; everyone else (other than the boss) is under suspicion for corruption and has been suspended, so I've been awarded temporary promotion. Lucky me. I'm now, temporarily, whilst I'm on secondment, Detective Inspector Scott Dempsey.

It's got a nice ring to it, that. I should be pleased, really, but this could quite easily go either way; it's going to make or completely destroy my career and, just to rub salt in the wounds, nobody seems to be taking my theory seriously. We've got five unsolved murders, all with seemingly obvious motives, and a list of suspects longer than a whale's dick. They've all been tortured and the actual cause of death can't be properly identified for a lot of them. Up until now, they've been treated as separate incidents; fuck, one of them is even reported as solved, arrest made and case closed, but I'm working on the theory that they're linked, that it's one person. In each case, the victim has been tortured, and with each progressing case the method is more and more bizarre. In some circumstances, it's even funny in a sick kind of way.

I need to think it through properly though; there's little point in raising my thoughts again to the boss until I've got some serious weight in the argument to back it up, or he'll just give me a bollocking for wasting my time and add some other boring shit to my workload to fatten my day out. It needs to be... conclusive, obvious, and nailed on. Thanks to Tim's slapdash approach to working, I've got a bunch of files that could take an age to work through, though. There's at least four years' worth of material here and it's in a right old mess.

One of the things I need to figure out is the motivation for these crimes. Is this person some kind of real-life bloody superhero? Christ knows that the world's a better place for each person that's been killed not being in it. Or could they be just using their victim's wrongs as an excuse to kill people in weird and fantastical ways? Whatever it is, I can't see them stopping any time soon; if it really is one person they're getting too good at it now. With each progressive murder, the torture is more bizarre and the cause of death even less obvious.

I think the best course of action for me to take is going to be to try and question this reporter woman, Julie Newton. She's been missing for two weeks and usually by that time a body has turned up. There are a couple of exceptions to this rule, but I always had a feeling she'd still be alive. I firmly believed that Tim didn't have anything to do with her disappearance. He's a pretty straight-up bloke, from my experience, although if Julie's article is accurate, maybe he's not everything I've held him up to be. The thing is, though, I just can't figure out why, if I'm right about the link, she would be a target. Surely she would be on his side? She was kind of a vigilante herself. Unless she was considered competition, perhaps; there's always a chance of that. Perhaps there was some deep-rooted jealousy there about the fact that she can print what she wants, for everyone to see, and pop her name at the bottom of a piece to show off how good she is, whereas my guy has to do everything anonymously.

I call him 'guy' because they generally are – serial killers, that is. They're usually white blokes aged thirty to fifty. Filter it down further and you get two types of serial killer, the organised and the disorganised. Each poses its own unique problems and opportunities. Disorganised killers kill on impulse and are reasonably sloppy when it comes to covering up their tracks, but because they're so disorganised, you don't know where they're going to hit next.

My guy's definitely in the organised category; these people plan who they're going to kill, intricately. They'll usually have their initial meeting with the victim organised, structured and (in their own mind) rehearsed in advance. A bit like a confidence trickster, they'll act out a role in order to get their victim to trust them. Once they've built up the trust, they'll generally take the victim somewhere to carry out the kill. Somewhere private where they can do exactly what they need to do with them. A famous example of this is Ted Bundy. He'd pretend to have a broken arm or be injured, and when a woman came to lend a hand, they'd be dragged off to some pre-prepared place, then killed and raped.

It's not as simple as just the one filter, though. Once you've established the first point, there is another load of categories to filter through again, and it's here where I'm unsure which our guy is. The only one I'm pretty certain he's not, is 'gain motivated'; he doesn't seem to be doing this for status or financial reasons. However, that still leaves me with a handful of categories he could easily slot into.

'Visionaries' believe their actions are justified. They believe they are on some sort of mission, usually claiming to hear voices or be doing something for supernatural reasons. My guy could easily fall into this category, as everyone he's killed deserved what they got. They were all bastards. He perhaps thinks he's some sort of superhero or something.

This links closely in with 'Missionaries', who go for cleansing a certain type of victim (again thinking they're doing good). They may target a single ethnic or social group.

'Hedonistic' killers kill for the pleasure of killing and nothing else. It gives them some kind of sexual pleasure, even if only subconsciously. The victims may not display any signs of abuse, but when the crime is broken down into sections, if there seems to be a retentive layer of creative and bizarre detail attached to any single point, hedonism is definitely an option – and looking at the torture carried out on some of these victims, there's a big fat tick in the hedonistic box as far as I can see.

Then, finally, there are 'Power and Control' killers, who do exactly what it says in the description. Their motivation often stems from unresolved issues surrounding their childhood; their killing may sometimes seem sexual or ritualistic. Once again, this description seems to fit.

My problem here is obvious; without determining which specific category my guy falls into, I can't get enough detail together to build a profile and present my findings, to get the relevant funding and support to apprehend him before he kills again. Conversely, without the relevant funding to employ a properly trained psychological profiler, I'm likely to fall flat on my face.

I need to do some digging. I also need to do something about my desk. It looks like a bomb's hit it and, as if that wasn't enough, I need to get to work on putting the key information from these files into my PC. I mean, they're already logged in the police files and everything, but they're all logged as separate cases. Tim had been helping me in collecting the information, but I don't know how he managed to keep track of everything properly, working from these stupid files. It's like the Dark Ages. This could turn into the biggest murder hunt in this area since the Yorkshire Ripper and Tim's learned bugger all. They'd have caught the Ripper a lot sooner if they'd have been better organised.

I can deal with all that when I get back, though. I'm here at the hospital now and the doctors have told me I can speak with Julie as long as I don't upset or aggravate her. I think they assume that, just because she wrote that article, we all have it in for her, but they're wrong. I couldn't care less about that. I've got a bigger fish to fry.

Holme Bridge Hospital is a grim place to be, it stinks of rancid old piss and death. The walls and old rooms look like something from a survival horror video game and the gardens surrounding it are covered in twisted, weathered trees. The only thing you can hear here, other than the repetitive bleeping of the monitors attached to everyone, is the old windows rattling in the wind.

I came in here once as a child when I had Testis. I suppose a place is bound to seem scary and spooky to me when my first memory of it is being rushed in, anaesthetised, operated on and waking up on an old creepy ward with balls bigger than my fist, and an angry line of stitches up the front of them. Nasty, that Testis; it happens to loads of lads around puberty, when your balls start dropping. What happens is, they drop wrong and start to twist around each other. You can't feel it much at first, it's kind of a dull ache, but it gets worse quick. I plucked up the courage to get my knackers out in front of my mum and when she saw the wrinkled lump of flesh that used to be my ball bag, she called the emergency doctor out. He spotted what it was straight away and didn't even bother hanging around calling and waiting for an ambulance; he carefully carried me to his car and rushed me straight in here. Apparently, what happens to a lot of kids is they ignore it and eventually the pain stops. It stops because they've twisted so tight, they've snapped off, and it's only when they come to trying to have kids later in life that they realise they've been firing blanks for years.

The doctor who's walking towards me is looking at me with a strange expression that seems to be a mixture of repugnance and bewilderment, which isn't surprising, really, seeing that I've just realised that I'm sitting here cupping my balls. I move my hands quickly away whilst he tells me I'm allowed to go in and see her.

En route, I'm reminding myself to stick to one line of questioning: her kidnapping. Don't get involved in a conversation about anything else and definitely don't divulge anything that could be considered incriminating. Not that I even know anything that could be considered that way, but I'm fully aware of what journalists are like.

As I pass one of the private rooms, I hear a shout and I can hear the constant bleep of a heart monitor that's advising the worst. I quickly rush towards the door and open it, only to be ordered out by a seriously stressed-out-looking doctor struggling to revive a patient who has so many tubes and wires coming off him that he looks like some kind of cyborg. I consider flashing my police ID card but can't see much point. What can I do to help? And anyway, I've got an interview to conduct. I make a sharp exit and continue down the corridor. It takes long enough for me to hear the heart monitor's drone turn into an irregular series of beeps.

I approach her door and stand outside to gather my thoughts, once again reminding myself to think before I speak. Then I open the door quietly and slowly, trying to take a little time to take in the surroundings. She has a private room and I'm quite surprised at the mod cons in here. Her bed looks like it has more electronic controls on it than one of those mad scientist's labs in the old cartoons, and there's a phone connected to a small LCD television, coming off it on a large moveable metal bracket.

She turns to look at me and I can't quite place her expression. Confusion? Resentment? I take a breath as I sit down beside her bed, and decide to wait quietly and let her open the conversation in her own time. No sense in rushing her; if I mess this up and she doesn't trust me, this could cause me more problems than it solves.

PSYCHOTIC
JACK WILKINSON

I wasn't always this way. For years, I suppressed my genius; I tucked it away deep down inside and tried to ignore it, but eventually I came to realise that my uncle needed a hand in dying and those creative cogs clicked properly into gear. In retrospect, it was magical seeing my theory becoming reality for the first time, even if I did manage to make a right old fucking mess of it.

I don't really want to go into my reasons why in too much detail, as I'll no doubt just end up repeating myself as I try to explain, but he was a very bad man, he did things to me when I was a child. Slowly but surely, he wormed his way into my affections and built up my trust, then he abused that trust for years. I never stood up to him, never questioned him and never told a soul. As I grew older, he became less and less interested in me and it all faded away so gradually that, over time, I pretty much forgot.

I got on with my life as normal, which mainly included going about my business secretly thinking of new and wonderful ways to mutilate, torture, maim, poison, immobilise, persecute, torment, disfigure, contaminate and finally execute someone. They were just thoughts, though; we all have them, it's just that mine ended up as a little bit more than a passing fancy or fleeting notion. Somewhere deep down, I truly wanted to do it. I wanted to see what would happen and I was curious to see if it would be like it was on the television. I knew it wouldn't be fair to do it on just anybody, though; I needed to pick someone that truly deserved it. I'm not an animal.

Then, in November six or seven years ago, it hit me like a sledgehammer. My sister gave birth to my nephew and the memories of what my uncle had done all those years ago came flooding back to me. There wasn't a chance I was going to let him do it to anybody else, so I got my thinking cap on and racked my brains to sift through some of the highlights of my ideas over the years and find one that would seem suitable for a bastard like him. I needed to access my archive…

At this time, my cellar didn't house a room. That was born out of necessity later on. It simply hid everything that I might be considered weird for having, like my porn, for example. There was nothing in there that was illegal, mind, it's just that there was so fucking much of it that I didn't have room left in the house. I also kept all the small scraps of paper that I'd scribbled my torture and killing ideas onto down there. I opened the old wooden hatch and made my way down the stairs.

It used to be awful in there, old brick exposed walls, no heating, and a single bulb hanging from the roof to illuminate it that swung softly with the icy breeze that seemed to constantly swirl around the room, kicking the dust up and around everywhere and making it hard to breathe. Not that I ever got any thanks from any of my victims later on for addressing these issues. I even put a bed in. The ungrateful fucking twats.

So, I trundled around, grasping at the odd piece of paper that floated past my feet as I made my way to the far end of the room where I'd boxed most of my ideas. I tried reading some of the loose scribblings, but my scrawls seemed mostly illegible; I'd probably written them when I was pissed or something. That's probably why they ended up on the floor rather than in the box.

One thing that I do remember very distinctly is that once I actually got to the box, it dawned on me just how at peace my mind must have been for quite a while before my sister's bambino arrived. Probably even before her pregnancy. The box was thick with dust so I mustn't have been down that end for ages. I mean, sure, I'd been down, but I kept all of the porn at the bottom of the stairs and mustn't have had to venture to the far end for a long while; this surprised me quite a bit at the time.

Anyway, I lifted the lid and began sifting through my ideas, some of which, although very good, were just plain impractical. 'The Lung Parachute' was a classic example of creative flair over practicality. I loved the idea of pushing someone out of a plane with two small hooks pushed into their back and between their ribs, so that as they fell, their lungs tore through their skin and opened out as they caught the wind, allowing someone to suffocate as they gently plummeted towards the earth with their lungs acting as a parachute, but it just wasn't a realistic option. I didn't know if it would work, for a start, and I didn't have an accomplice with a plane and, more importantly, I'm scared of flying and afraid of fucking heights so it was right out of the question.

Something straightforward was needed. Something easy. And then I found it… 'The Freezing Ball Castration'. It was perfect for my uncle in so many ways that I'm surprised it never occurred to me to do it sooner. The premise was, as all good ideas are, unbelievably simple, but it would be so fantastically effective. Here's the idea: strap the victim (must be male obviously as you'll see) to a chair naked, put a small tub of cold water around his balls, lock him somewhere freezing cold and wait for the water to turn to ice, slowly crushing his fucking balls.

Here's the reason it was perfect: my uncle had a large café on the main road leading out of town as you head towards the motorway. He named it after himself; it was called *The Kiddy Fiddler*...That was a joke, obviously; it was called *Jacko's*. My mum used to drop me off there when I was little so he could keep an eye on me whilst she worked a second job. It worked out good for me; I was only five at the time and around the perimeter of the long, oblong dining room were video games; *Q-Bert, Crystal Castles, Pac Man, Bubble Bobble* and even the *Star Wars* game that you sat down in and piloted an X-Wing. I used to love it in there. My uncle would be serving behind the counter but he'd give me as many ten pence pieces as I wanted until closing time, to keep rolling in those machines. Then, once the shutters were down, he'd make me do the odd job for him to pay him back. It started off as just wiping down tables and emptying ashtrays, and over time ended up with him taking pictures of me being groped and sucking him off. The sick fucking bastard.

I remember the first time he touched me – and this is what makes this particular course of revenge and prevention so sweet. At the back of the café, through the back door and outside, was a huge walk-in freezer. He'd had a delivery of burgers this one particular day and I was helping him to carry them in. My memory of how we reached the following stage is a little hazy, but somehow, probably due to him shutting it, the door had closed and he thought we might be locked in. He struggled to try and get it open, but it wasn't working, apparently. I was scared and cold, but he came over and held me to keep me warm, then he touched me; he told me it would keep me warmer, and he told me to touch him and help keep him warm, too. That was the start of it all, probably about six years of abuse, progressively worse and then slowly fading to nothing. But it was in that freezer that he first abused me and it was in that freezer that I would castrate him and kill him. And learn an awful lot about the importance of planning and preparation in the process.

*

It was probably around early December when I decided to do it. It seemed like a perfect time as, in those couple of weeks before the immediate run-up to Christmas, the road quietened off at closing time; the village offered late night shopping and the usual rush of cars that would burn past between five and six o' clock, trickled across between six and nine. He closed early at this time of year because of how quiet it was, so I caught the bus up there straight after work. I couldn't drive at the time; driving was something else I had to do out of necessity rather than desire.

The bus was running on time for a change on that particular day and would have got me to the café too early, so I hopped off at the stop before and walked the rest of the way, calmly running through exactly what I was going to do in my head; knock him out, get the shutters down, drag him out the back and into the freezer, tie him to a chair, use one of the large, empty margarine tubs in which he used to store salad stuff to rest his cock and balls in, set up my webcam, and wait and watch from the warm comfort of the café's kitchen as he slowly got castrated and died.

Christ, if only it was so fucking simple. The first part of the plan, knock him out, was the first part to fail. I watched from the roadside with my coat pulled up to keep the cold out as he pulled the main two shutters that covered the front windows; then, as he moved across to do the one that covered the door, I ran over to him. He was taken aback to see me as it had been a long time. He didn't look concerned, though. Not a single shred of "Oh, my God, he's come back for revenge" crossed his face.

He just said, "Oh, hello lad, long time no see."

I felt my blood beginning to boil and had to clamp my jaw and clench my fists tight into themselves. Thankfully, he couldn't see them as one hand was in my pocket and the other was already grasping my laptop bag. I slowly counted to three in my head and, as I felt my body begin to relax again, I told him that I had something important to tell him. Once he'd invited me inside and closed the door, I dropped the laptop and punched him hard in the chin with everything I had.

In my naïve inexperience of an actual fight, I thought this would knock him out, but the old bastard took it, he barely flinched. I panicked and grabbed a glass ashtray from a table to the right of me but, before I could lift it, I found myself looking at the ceiling. It's weird because I was looking up at the ceiling before I actually realised that the wind had been knocked out of me by a severe blow to the ribs.

I spluttered and groaned like a fucking zombie as I rolled onto my side to gasp for breath, and as I did so, he lowered himself, squatting down, his fucking balls right in front of my face. I'd like to tell you what he was saying, but by this time the red mist had descended on my mind and the sight of his crotch motivated me to stop being such a fucking fanny and get on with it.

I pushed him over and he fell on the greasy floor. I dived on top of him and grabbed his straggly grey hair with both hands before sharply pulling up his head and then smashing it onto the tiles.

I kept hold of his hair and lifted his head up again. Blood was pissing out of the back of it and I began to worry that I'd killed him. That was, until the fucker started trying to wriggle out from under me. I quickly smashed his head down again, this time turning it to the side a bit to avoid making the wound any worse by repeating the impact in the same place. I pulled his head up again. He seemed knocked out this time.

I rested his head on the floor and checked the pulse in his neck; it was there, just. I knew I needed to stop the bleeding or he'd be fucking dead before I got the chance to exact my revenge. I also needed to wait long enough for him to wake up, as I wanted him to know what was going to happen to him.

The first thing I did was rifle through his pockets to find his keys, then I lowered the door shutter and locked us both in. I was unsure at this point whether the best course of action would be to address the wound, or get him to the freezer. I opted for the latter, knowing that if I could get him in there and securely strap him to a chair, I could clean up the blood whilst he was coming to.

I grabbed his legs and as I dragged him from the doorway back to the counter, a backwards 'C' shape of blood curled across the floor and around the table that had been in the way. I lifted the flap that allowed access to the back of the counter and the kitchen, and dragged him through. Once at the kitchen's back door, I grabbed his keys, opened it and walked to the outside freezer, checking as I did so to make sure nobody was around. I opened the door, went back through the kitchen and quickly pulled him out and into the freezer.

I needed a chair, so I got one from the café. It was hard work putting him onto it. I'd heard the term 'dead weight' before but had kind of let it wash over me; now I realised how accurate that phrase was. He was such a pain in the fucking arse to get on the chair, flopping around all over like a heavy human jelly. Then, once I'd finally managed to prop the old fucker on it and sit him up straight, I realised I had nothing to tie him up with.

I raced back to the kitchen, realising that I was seriously up against the clock. Would he wake up? Would he bleed to death? I needed to act fast, so I rifled through all the kitchen cabinets, furiously turfing out their contents all over the floor, and couldn't find a fucking thing that resembled a rope. I only had one option and that was to tie him up with tea towels and dish cloths, so I grabbed as many as I could carry and sprinted back to the freezer. He was still out cold and getting fucking colder. I carefully tied his legs to the chair legs, not using just one towel, but loads, all the way up to his knees. Then I tied his arms to the chair's back legs. He was now as secure as I could manage to get him. I used another towel on his head as a large bandage and ran inside to clean up. I left the kitchen and freezer doors open so I could hear if he woke up, and so he wouldn't freeze to death before I'd managed to carry out what I had in mind.

When I got back into the dining area, I sat down, feeling exhausted. This was not going as I had planned at all. I made a mental note that if there were a next time, I would need a safer, cleaner and easier way to knock someone out, and I should also make an inventory and ensure that I had all the necessary tools at my disposal before starting.

I glanced around at the mess and decided it could wait; the front of the café was secure so there was no way anyone was getting in and I needed to get his bollocks in some water fast.

I went through to the kitchen and filled an empty margarine tub with water as planned, and headed to the freezer, where I placed it carefully on the floor beside him and started to unbutton his trousers. I'd not made it easy for myself; I really should have just taken them off before I tied him up. It was a fucking chore but I managed to get them down to his knees. Going through all this and looking at his wrinkly old cock brought back awful memories, but I tried to cancel them out by telling myself that after this, he'd never be able to do what he did again.

I picked up the margarine tub, lifted his cock and balls, gently placed the tub between his legs and dropped his meat and two veg into it. Then I ran back to get my webcam, set it up on a shelf diagonally right and down from where I'd put him, then retreated to the kitchen, locking the doors on my way past, so that I could watch my work unfold on the laptop screen. At least I'd thought to get the wireless webcam, otherwise I'd have been watching from outside the freezer in the cold.

As I sat watching, it dawned on me that it might take longer for the water to freeze than for him to die of hypothermia. This pissed me off. I checked to see if there was an internet connection anywhere so that I could find out, but there wasn't one. I'd just have to make sure I kept him alive.

I sat watching for what seemed like ages and was starting to get pretty bored, but then he started to come around. His head began to wobble and I could see an expression of pain on his face. Yes! This was it. I was finally going to get something fucking right, or so I thought. He started wriggling and wobbling and he looked like he might rock himself off the chair. I needed to secure it, make sure he couldn't wobble it over.

I sprinted into the freezer and had a look around. He was screaming at me and pleading with me to let him go, but I didn't even acknowledge him. At least my presence there stopped him from struggling for a while and, as I searched around, his screams faded into sobs and then he did something I wasn't expecting. He apologised.

I paced back towards him and stood in front him, looking down on the broken excuse of a man that used to prey on me as a child. I think he expected me to say something to him like, "Oh well, that's okay then," and let him go free. I said nothing, though; nothing at all. I just moved to the side of the chair, grasped it by the front and back legs at the bottom and carefully slid it until it was backed up against the wall of the freezer.

His sobs turned into screams again and he started to shake. I could see the water in the tub beginning to splash around and I started to get aggravated. I needed something heavy to wedge up against the other side of the chair to stop him wobbling it over, so I went to the back of the freezer and found an outer box of chips. It was around the same width and depth as a washing machine but around a third of the height. It would have to do. It was too heavy to lift, so I slid it across and wedged it on the other side of the chair.

Then I checked the tub. There was still just enough water in it to do the job, but if he kept wriggling, that would change in no time. As I watched him struggle, potentially ruining my plan, my patience ran out and I snapped. I charged back into the kitchen and went rooting through the cupboards and drawers. I knew what I needed; I'd seen it in there earlier when I was looking for something to tie him up with. It wasn't going to be pretty, but it'd do the trick.

I found it. The toolkit was in a cupboard with the cleaning materials. I grabbed what I needed and headed back to the freezer. As he saw me coming, he screamed. I'd never heard a man properly scream before – I'm desensitised to it nowadays. He was helpless. As I approached him, he begged and pleaded but it fell on deaf ears. I reached into the tub and pinched the front part of his tight, cold, curled-up scrotum, being careful not actually to clamp either of his balls, and pulled it. It was tougher than I expected, like old chewing gum. I stretched it tight but as soon as I released it, it immediately started to retreat back into its original prune-like state and I realised I'd need to be quick. I stretched it again, grabbed a nail from my pocket and skewered it, then released my grip, grabbed the hammer from my other pocket and began to tap gently. He screamed again, more loudly this time. Again, I didn't acknowledge him. I needed to be careful not to damage his balls; hitting them with a hammer was too good for him. I tapped a little harder and a little faster, until his scrotum and the tub were nailed securely to the chair.

I needed to top up the water as there wasn't nearly enough in there to do the job anymore. I thought about it briefly and decided to use some of the frost from the wall of the freezer; it would be colder, speed up the process, I thought. I pinched fingerfuls from the wall and dropped it in. Once there was enough, I changed the angle of the camera and got out of the freezer, closing it behind me, and retreated to the warmth of the kitchen to finally enjoy my work.

He was struggling but only a little. I assumed that he was either exhausted, or it hurt too much, or ideally, that he'd realised that he had best just do what I intended or things could get worse. After fifteen minutes or so he began shivering, really badly, so that I began to think my fear of hypothermia kicking in before the task had been done was becoming a reality. I needed to keep him alive, warm enough to not die from the cold, but not so warm that his body heat would prevent the water from freezing. It was a puzzle.

I boiled the kettle, soaked an apron in the scalding water; removed it with some tongs and ran back to the freezer. I waved it around a little to cool it off and then tied it tightly around the towel I'd already put on his head to stop the bleeding. This seemed to perk him up almost immediately. He became coherent and started to tell me that if I would just let him go, he wouldn't say a word and nobody would ever need to know. He begged and pleaded.

Again, I didn't speak, just glanced down at the water, which looked to be coming along nicely, left him and went back to the kitchen to watch on the laptop. He looked fucking funny, sat half naked, balls in a margarine tub, nailed to a cheap plastic chair with a fucking apron bundled on his head like the world's biggest turban, with so much steam coming off it, it looked like his head was on fire. I wasn't laughing for long, though. He slowly began to look as if he was losing the will to live and eventually he hung his head backwards. Had he died?

Jesus! This was a pain in the fucking arse. I grabbed the scissors that were strewn on the floor from my earlier cupboard-rooting efforts and marched back in, reckoning that a couple of little stabs to the thighs should wake him up. When I lifted his head, I found that he wasn't dead, he was simply destroyed, definitely lost the will, head hung loose, eyes closed and accepting his fate. I finally lost my cool and shouted at him, "Open your fucking eyes!"

He said nothing. I shouted again and he started to laugh – the cunt started fucking laughing at me!

"Fuck you," he slurred, "I'm not playing this fucking game anymore, just kill me… Oh, that's right you can't, because it'll ruin your fucking little game. Well, fuck you. I'm not playing."

I lost it then. I lifted his head. "Not playing?" I shouted "Not fucking playing?" Then I pushed his head back, took the scissors and carefully removed his eyelids. It was difficult because he struggled. I tried to start at the far corner but I couldn't pull the skin out to get the edge of the scissors in, it was like each corner was glued or something. Eventually, I just pulled his top lids outwards, did a single snip straight up the middle and then just grabbed the loose flaps and fucking ripped them clean off with my fingers. Once again, this backfired. The blood was pissing into his eyes and he couldn't blink it away; anything I did at that point would just have made his vision worse. I'd made an almighty mess of something that had seemed so perfect in theory.

I couldn't take it anymore so I took the scissors and cut off his tiny shrivelled-up penis, then I removed the nail with the claw end of the hammer, took the scissors again and cut off his fucking balls as well, then I shoved them all in his mouth and held his jaw closed. I nipped his nose with my fingers to restrict his breathing and held him tight until he choked and suffocated on his own fucking cock, the way I had nearly done all those years ago. As I felt the struggle and life drain out of him, I felt something bubbling up inside me. I couldn't feel the cold of the freezer anymore. I breathed in deeply though my nose and felt a euphoria I had never felt before, or imagined, or experienced could be possible. I let go of him and my breathing stopped and a blackness crept in from the outside of my vision, slowly intensifying with the rush, accompanied by a quiet but intense ringing in my ears, and then I collapsed.

I don't know how long I was out for, not more than a couple of seconds though, I think. As I composed myself, the realisation of everything I'd just done hit me and I felt awful, like I'd been enjoying fucking some ugly munter, shot my muck and then looked at the fucking mess of a bird that was glaring longingly up at me, and realised the mistake I'd made. But this was a billion times more intense.

I also realised that I hadn't been wearing any gloves and I'd touched every cupboard, utensil and worktop in the kitchen, I'd scraped my finger across the walls of the freezer, there was blood all over the dining area and my DNA would be all over his fucking face. I had some cleaning and disposal work to do. I would leave the body, though; neatly place him in the centre of the freezer. I wanted whoever found him to be repulsed by him. It was all he deserved.

ESCAPING
DAD

As he drifts slowly back into his own conscious mind, he's reminded of the people, places and events that shaped his life and brought him to where he is now. The most powerful image of all is that of his father. He doesn't remember his mother at all. He knows what she looked like from photographs and other people's descriptions, but any actual memories are gone save for a few patchy, hazy bits of nonsensical randomness.

His memory begins at her funeral. It was a tiny venue that, under most circumstances, looked full by default but on this occasion it still managed to look empty. They were a tiny family, just him, his father and grandmother. The small hall bounced the echoes of the priest's booming voice around the room and he cried as the coffin at the front moved slowly into the darkness that concealed the furnace. Not because he was upset himself, really. More because he'd never seen his grandmother or father cry before and they were sat either side of him, weeping uncontrollably. He couldn't understand why; he knew about heaven and thought that surely his mummy would be happy there. After the service, his dad kept telling him that everything would be okay, but he was only just four years old and so young he didn't really understand what he meant. He did a good job of looking upset, mainly because it made everybody else feel better, but he himself didn't really feel anything more than a little bit confused.

Once the funeral was over, he and his father went back home. His grandmother had offered to come with them, but his dad had told her that he wanted some time alone with his son. As he looks back on it now, it seems pretty obvious that he just used that as an excuse to cry his eyes out properly again, this time without an audience. He'd told his son to stay in his room but he quietly crept out to see what was going on. His father was sitting in their dimly lit living room with his head in his hands and a couple of empty cans of strong lager around his feet. He can't remember now if this is the point when his father's drinking started, or if he'd always been at it, but that was the first time he'd actually noticed. He would come to notice it more and more as the year went on.

The next stand-out thing that burns through his memory is when he started school. He was really looking forward to it and excited to be on his way. His father was driving him in his new Datsun Cherry Coupe. It was scorching hot for a September and they had the windows down. He was reaching his arm out completely straight with his fingers spread out and rotating his hand left to right, feeling the cool wind brush through his fingers.

His dad was bopping up and down to the song that was pounding tinnily through the stereo, some electro pop; he had a massive huge grin on his face, he looked happy. That was the only time he would ever see him smile in such a way, and that was the happiest he would ever see him be.

His father dropped him off and he had to walk across the school's hard asphalt playground. It seems huge to him in this particular memory, and decidedly less wobbly than it will when he remembers his teens. He joined a queue of other children waiting to go inside. Most of them seemed much bigger than him; he'd later find out that he was born only two days off starting school a year later.

He was the last child to arrive, right at the back of the queue. They all filed in and sat down in the gym, where they got told which class they would be in. He looked around the room. He'd never seen so many children in one place at one time. He wondered what all the strange apparatus he could see tucked away and strapped to walls was, and paid attention to which classes were being called out by the teacher, and the corresponding pupils. He tried to decide if the ones that ended up in his class looked friendly. He was in Class Two. As the children were instructed to get to their feet, and were asked to follow their respective teachers to their classrooms, he was so interested in his surroundings that he wasn't taking notice of where he was going and he knocked his head on a bookshelf and started crying. All the other kids laughed at him and he suddenly felt something that he'd never felt before; pure embarrassment and insecurity. This made him cry even harder. His teacher, Mr Martin, came to his aid, but ended up making it a thousand times worse by telling him in front of the other kids that there was no need to cry as his daddy would be coming back to get him soon. He was so distraught and embarrassed that he could barely even breathe, never mind speak to try and explain that he didn't want his dad, he'd just hurt his head.

Things went from bad to worse in the afternoon. The pupils in the class were boiling down old wax crayons to pour them into moulds and make candles to take home to their parents, and the teacher asked the class if anybody knew where wax came from. Eager to try and save face from his earlier crying incident, he excitedly thrust his hand into the air to answer the question. He was relieved when he was picked, but his enthusiasm soon changed to embarrassment and insecurity again when his answer caused the rest of the class, and the teacher, to laugh at him once more. He couldn't understand why, because "your ears" was surely the correct response.

Foggy, hazy patches of being bullied and his dad's drinking swirl around like a washing machine full of poison and pain. There isn't much there other than the memory of them being there; he's discarded the details, spared himself the hurt of the actual facts. Plus, his memory needs that space for far worse incidents.

One of these burns through so hard and clear, it's as if it were branded onto his brain. He was around six years of age. By this point, his father's drinking had become out of control. Not all of the time, but definitely a lot of the time. He was a binge alcoholic, sober and alright for a few days but that was merely the calm before the tornado. He was like a timebomb of aggression and violence, ticking, waiting to explode. Once he did, for the next day, days, or even week, he would drink constantly. Throughout this time, his son was neglected, left completely on his own without food, or used as a punch bag.

Also during this time, what seemed like countless numbers of women would pass through the house, some nice, some not so nice. All drunk. It would always end in shouting and yelling, on the odd occasion kicking and screaming, then this one particular day it all went a bit too far.

He could hear them downstairs. There had been a couple of loud bangs, he imagined they must have been throwing things at each other. He was terrified and did as he always did; climbed out of his bed in silence, quietly crawled across his bedroom and climbed into his toy box.

He heard another bang, this one even louder, followed by a large yelp from his father, and then it went quiet... too quiet. He climbed out of the box and made his way slowly to his bedroom door; where he carefully lowered the handle and pulled the door towards him to peer through the gap. He couldn't see a thing but he could hear a sort of tapping, thudding noise, an irregular knocking. His heart began to pound and he could feel each beat throughout his entire body, but he wanted to know what it was. He opened the door a little more and squeezed through the smallest gap he thought he could get away with; he knew that with one creak he could be in big trouble so he didn't want to push the door any further open than he needed to. He carefully passed across the hall and reached the top of the stairs. The noise was louder now. His fear had been replaced by an intense curiosity by this time, so he started to descend the stairs slowly and carefully, one foot at a time, one stair at a time.

As he reached about a third of the way down, he peeped through a gap in the banisters and found that he could see through the open living room door. He couldn't see much from that angle, just a tiny corner of the room. The TV in the corner was on, but wasn't tuned in properly. The picture was flickering and, as it was the only source of light in the room, it made it look like a scene from an old black and white movie.

Two sets of feet could be seen jutting toward the doorway, one facing up and between them his father's, facing down. They were moving a small amount, rubbing against the carpet, but it wasn't them that was making the noise. He crept down another couple of stairs and could now see both sets of feet, and the ankles and up to the knees. It didn't seem strange to him that they were unclothed at this stage, but as he descended further and could see his father moving up and down from the knee as he thrust, he got confused as to what he was seeing.

He made his way to the bottom and stood frozen outside the doorway, staring inside. He could clearly see his sweating father having sex with one of his conquests, not that he knew what it was at that age. He could also see that whilst he was doing this, his father had a tight grasp of the woman's throat. He didn't understand what he was looking at, his father choking some woman whilst writhing on her like an animal. Paralysed, he stood and watched whilst his father squeezed every last inch of life from the woman lying beneath him. He saw his father stop, remove his hands from her throat and begin to move, then, realising that he may be in for a similar fate if he got seen, he turned and just as carefully as he had descended, made his way back up the stairs.

He could hear more noise from below now, pounding and banging. He heard the living room door slam shut and breathed a sigh of relief as the sounds of banging became instantly muffled and he knew his father was inside the room rather than outside.

He was terrified. A million thoughts raced through his young brain as to what might happen to him. After he reached out to slowly open his bedroom door, he glanced across the hall to the telephone table, then knew what he had to do. He approached it, lifted the receiver as quietly as he could and dialled the number he had been taught to dial at school in case anything went wrong, 999. Once the operator answered, he whispered, "Please can you come and get me? My daddy's just killed a lady and I think he's going to kill me."

*

His memory drifts towards an interview in a cold room with a policeman and two women. He's too young at this point to understand their roles, which were that of a child psychologist and a solicitor. He answers all their questions as honestly as he can, understanding very little of the potential consequences of his words in terms of what the legal system would do to his father. During the trial, he would hear 'auto-asphyxiation' mentioned by the defence to justify and excuse the murder; not that he understood what that meant at that point.

He remembers the anger and hatred in his father's eyes as the verdict was delivered. Burning through him, eyebrows narrowed and eyes widened. He remembers his dad kicking up a fuss and lunging towards him. He knocked the woman transcribing the courtroom conversations over, her small machine falling on top of her as she went. Three policemen wrestled him to the floor and, as he struggled and writhed trying to stop them from handcuffing him, he looked at his son and screamed across the courtroom, "It was an accident!"

JUSTICE
PUZZLE

I can see her sitting just across the way from me; it's like seeing her for the first time all over again. Her long, flowing, strawberry blonde hair is draped behind one shoulder and over the other, framing a beauty so perfect that I'm transfixed. Her large, hypnotic, deep brown eyes almost burn through me and her plump lips seem to be calling my name. I slowly glance down to admire her dress. It's a lilac, low cut, strappy number that clings to her everywhere I would want it to and flows down to just below the knee, and because she is sitting down with her legs bent, I can see her knees in the flesh, poking through just between where the dress ends and the velvety blue high boots begin. It sounds stupid, I know, but just looking at them fills me with an overwhelming lust.

I know I should be bothered about the fact that my wife is seated next to me whilst these feelings flit through my mind, but at this precise moment I couldn't care less. I continue to stare at her perfect frame but the other people at the table with us don't notice. Nor does anyone else in this trendy wine bar. As I pause my admiration and glance around, I realise that there isn't a sound of any kind coming from anyone or anywhere. All around me I can see people talking, chinking glasses, raising toasts and even dancing, but there's not a peep, not a single sound from any of it and then it dawns on me… I can do whatever I want.

I grab her by the hand and rush outside into what appears to be a familiar looking city street, although I can't pinpoint the reason why. I decide we need to check into a hotel and, as we charge together through the subtly changing lanes, I see the flickering neon lights of a huge casino. It has a name but I can't read it, the words look like a jumbled mess. It seems closer now and then I'm inside it, begging with the guy on reception to find me a room, whilst he insists that this is an impossibility.

Eventually my persuasion pays off and I'm given a key, but as I open the door, the room unfolds into a huge bar area with a large, busy roulette table in the centre. The bed I need seems like an eternity away at the back of the room, underneath a window the size of a cinema screen that overlooks the entire city. The fact that it's so far away encourages rather than disappoints me, so I grab her hand and we charge towards the bed. Once there, I lay her down on it and simply stand for a moment, looking down at the beauty that lies before me, before grabbing her left breast. I gently squeeze; it feels so real. I kiss her lips and, as I do so, I rip open the top of her dress. I look down at her small but perfect breasts and I move down to kiss them, at the same time pulling up her skirt. I glance down again and then I'm interrupted, it's the fucking reception guy, he's telling me I can't do this here, and for some bizarre reason I listen to him and do as he says.

My lust turns into anger and I awaken frustrated. I look at my alarm clock; I've woken up before it goes off again. I could have another hour's sleep but what would be the point? I'd only end up back in the dream again and not be able to fuck her, like always. As I exit my bedroom and head downstairs to the kitchen, I can't help but feel upset. I know it sounds stupid but I'm in love with her. With every inch of my body and soul. Sometimes I get to see her every night and other times I won't see her for weeks on end. It's a complicated relationship. Sometimes I question whether leaving my wife was the right thing to do, but I knew even then that because my heart belonged to someone else, I was living a lie by staying with her, even if that someone else didn't exist in a physical sense.

As I put on the kettle and stare out of my back window into the garden, I can't help but notice what looks like melons growing there, and an old tramp sitting by a fire in the far corner. The tramp stares straight at me and says something and I notice that there isn't any noise. Fuck! I must still be asleep. I try to open my eyes and engage with my conscious body but I can't; I'm trapped in it, lying there, knowing full well I'm asleep but unable to move. I'm no longer in the kitchen, I'm now firmly in my body attached to the bed, but I can't communicate with my limbs. It's like being trapped in a human-shaped prison. I summon everything I have in me to try and yell, but little more than a whimper passes my lips. I begin to panic and my heart rate quickens. I've been through this so many times and every time it terrifies me. Once again, I try to move. I need to start with something simple, a finger, or my hand. I concentrate hard and then, with every inch of strength I have in me, I try to move my hand, but it won't work. I begin to cry, out of sheer frustration more than the fear, and as I do so, my alarm saves me.

The shock of it going off jolts me from being trapped in my subconscious to coming wide awake. I'm back. I go to rub my eyes and they're dry. It wasn't this me that had been crying at all; it was the other me, the one in the dreams that gets to do all the weird stuff. Is he me, or is he his own person? Part of me but not? Could my reality be his dream? Maybe that's it.

Perhaps, if I can do something worthwhile in my conscious state, I can finally have her. This encourages me to drag my arse out of bed and get to work; I've got a killer to catch.

*

When I arrive at work, I decide the best thing to do first is consolidate the information, or lack thereof, that I carefully extracted from Julie Newton the previous day. It was like pulling teeth. She clearly has a lot of trust issues when it comes to the police, as the first thing she said to me was, "There are only two types of copper, a new copper and a bent copper. Which are you?" Mind you, after reading her article, if it pans out to be true, I can see why she's so cynical. Listen to this:

A terrified young boy aged no more than fourteen cowered and shook as he told of his horrific ordeal.

He, like countless others before him, had been shipped over from small depressed villages on the outskirts of Poland to be sold as a slave to the highest bidder.

Every day children, some as young as six, are lured away from their parents with the promise of a better life, exclusive education and guarantee of a future career, only to be auctioned off to the highest bidding paedophile, and who is responsible? Our own police force.

Throughout my investigation, I discovered that the majority of our local CID as well as key personnel from HM Customs and Excise at Hull ferry port and Leeds Bradford Airport were responsible for this atrocity.

DI Tim Morris justified his actions to another implicated colleague (Inspector Charles Clarke) as a preventative measure to protect the children of Holme Bridge who had been failed by the legal system, and bragged about how easy it was to find customers as their names and addresses were all neatly stored in police files.

This sickening story runs deeper than anyone could have imagined as the police are re-investing their substantial ill-gotten funds into controlling the supply chain of illegal drugs into the Yorkshire area. This was once again justified as a means to ensure that the drug-taking public of the area were kept safe with monitored product and the dealers could all be properly monitored and tracked.

Full Story On Page 9.

It's twisted. I hope to God she's wrong, I truly do. After speaking to her, it does seem as if the circumstances surrounding her abduction and imprisonment are linked with some of the others and it definitely gives some very serious weight to my serial killer theory. As long as I can convince the boss that Tim definitely didn't have anything to do with it, I think it must be only a matter of time now before I get the funding I need to form a team to catch this bastard.

My biggest issue is getting it before he kills again. This guy isn't going to be happy that Julie Newton's abduction didn't culminate in some torture and killing, and he's going to need a fix soon. Why did he let her go, though? I think if I can figure that out, I stand a chance of trying to pinpoint the next person on his hit list. The only thing the others have in common is the seemingly endless list of potential suspects that surrounds them. There's Duncan Jameson, a solicitor that legally defended a lot of the paedophiles that have now been rumbled by Julie Newton's story; the parts of his autopsy report that aren't technical mumbo jumbo make for pretty grim reading. Try this for size:

EXTERNAL EXAMINATION:
The body is that of a 5ft 11inches, 12 Stone 4lbs male who appears to be the recorded age of 37. The body is naked. No clothing or other articles were received with the body. The scalp is covered in thick brown hair with flecks of grey.

Blah… blah…. Blah… Here we go.

Small scars varying in width from 2mm to 7mm cover the entire body, face and legs. They appear to be randomly scattered. Cause of scarring is unobvious. Possibly a small blade such as a razor blade or Stanley knife.

Horrible. It looked even worse than it sounds. Literally from head to toe he had been slashed, although there was no real sign of struggle. For someone to have caused that damage to someone else, you would have thought they would have had to restrain them somehow. Around some of the scars were circular bruises, some so close to each other that they bled into one. Really weird. The guy died from his blood loss. He had been administered with aspirin which had caused his blood to thin out.

The next victim was John Goodchild, a white collar criminal who laundered money but kept slipping through our fingers. His blood had thickened so much that he was like a human mannequin. When his body was discovered, the killer had managed to preserve the complete look of sheer agony and fear on his face. His body was on the floor, face-up, legs bunched up to his chest and cradled by his arms. We don't have the first clue as to how he did it.

The next one was Akbar Aslam, a radical Muslim who had been suspected of being instrumental in the recruiting and, I suppose, brain-washing of a number of young Muslims in the area. He had a fresh scar running from his neck to his torso and when he was opened up during the autopsy, pages from the Koran relating to peace and goodwill to men had been bonded to his insides. Perfectly. They weren't saturated with blood as you would expect, they were easily readable, like a textbook wallpapering of his insides. Once again, I have absolutely no idea how he managed to do it.

There are a couple of other deaths that could potentially be linked. There was a guy four years ago found frozen to death, choked, with his genitals removed and jammed halfway down his throat, but the profile is completely different and there seemed to be an obvious lack of control surrounding the injuries to the body. The flipside of this, and the reason I think it might have something to do with my man, is how pristine the location of the murder was. Real care and attention had been paid to ensure no clues were left behind. We all know the café where his body was found, we'd been in from time to time for food and it was a greasy hole, but it was immaculate when the body was found. There was also a young woman who had been mutilated in a sickening and disgusting fashion, but, again, it kind of seems against type.

There must be a link, something strong, something concrete, and Julie is the key to me tying it all together. She's so fucking obstructive and untrusting that I'm never going to get the information I need by conventional means. So here's what I'm thinking, and it could potentially spell disaster for me. I'm going to offer her exclusive, a one hundred per cent, no holds barred access to my entire investigation…

*

It's only an hour now since I asked her and I'm already beginning to realise that my good intentions are not going to be well received by the boss. As he caught sight of me walking towards my desk with her, he called me over for a word. He means fucking business, too; I'm not sat in his office, he's taken me into an interrogation room. The handle on the door moves and I mentally brace myself for his entrance.

"Scott, what the fuck is that bitch doing in here?"

As the question fires out of his angry mouth, I swear I can see steam coming out of his ears. He looks pretty angry at the best of times. Jim Kaney's about fifteen years older than me, I reckon, mid forties. His eyebrows form a point in the middle like those cartoon triangles that are used to accentuate a villainous look, and this is topped off by heavily pock-marked skin and a close crew cut. Perhaps that pitted skin is the reason he can be such a cunt. Probably had the piss taken out of him for having acne through school or something. I'm ready for this conversation, though. I know enough about psychology and the transition of human decision-making to get any conversation to go my way and I'm fairly sure that the training he received all those years ago will be nothing but a distant memory to him now.

"You're just going to have to trust me here, Guv, it's for the best," I say, trying to remain calm and unfazed.

"Trust you? Do you have any idea of the potential fucking hornet's nest you're playing with here? You've seen what she's done to this department already and you're not content with her simply fucking us over, now you want to invite her back for seconds! Are you a complete fucking idiot? I knew it was a mistake giving you this much responsibility. I thought you had something, Scott, I really thought you were up to this job. Obviously I was wrong."

"Guv," I say softly, in a calm, relaxed tone, hoping I can build some confidence, "think about it. She fucking hates us, she wants us to fail and if she has her own way with pursuing the stories she's been pursuing, she won't fucking stop until she's completely ruined everyone's faith in the police and got us all sacked."

He's lowered himself to my level now and the fury seems to be lifting from his face, to be replaced with what I hope is curiosity. I continue: "If I bring her in on my investigation, not only does she have a good story to tell, she'll also be more forthcoming with some information I need and see that some of us here do a fucking good job and genuinely care about this community. The cherry on the top of the cake is, while she's following me around, she's distracted from whatever she would have been digging around for. The only way any harm can come from her being involved in this with me is if, when she turns up, people around here aren't doing their job properly. Don't see this as a potential to ruin everything. See it as an opportunity to put it right, and if it does blow up, just sack me. It's not like things around here can get any worse, is it?"

He looks down and scratches the top of his head. I say nothing. He can make his own mind up here and it'll go my way if I keep shtum. If the silence takes ten minutes, I still won't say a word, I'll just wait patiently and confidently for him to agree with me.

PSYCHOTIC
THAT SOLICITOR GUY + JOHN GOODCHILD

Looking back over Julie Newton's story cheers me up immensely. I'd been so fixated with the *whom* behind her story that I'd barely focused on the *what* it was about. So here's what I'm thinking; I'm thinking Detective Inspector Tim Morris. Yes... He'll do nicely; he definitely deserves it, definitely looks like a random choice. Fuck me, there must be loads of people want that twisted fucker dead. I wonder what to do with him. I wish I had surgical knowledge because I'd love to sort of take him to pieces and put him back together again all jumbled up; that'd be fucking awesome. There must be a way; I've always managed to find a way to do everything before. Sometimes I know what I want the death to be, and have to figure out the journey, and other times I know what the journey is and need to figure out the death. That solicitor guy was a classic example of the latter.

I thought it'd be hilarious to kill someone by locking them into an enclosed environment and firing small rubber bouncy balls with razor blades in them at high speed into it, using the reverse blow of a leaf vacuum. I did it to him inside his own old coal bunker and set a webcam up in there so I could enjoy watching it afterwards. I chose him as a victim because he seemed to be getting every paedo going a fucking short or suspended sentence, and anyone that can do that had to have some kind of empathy for them; in my book, it made him just as bad.

It was with him that I found out how unpredictable chloroform is. After Uncle Jack hit back so hard when I tried to knock him out, I trawled the internet to find a way of buying chloroform so I could knock someone out quickly and simply like I'd seen on television. It was a lot easier to buy than I expected; it's used as a solvent, apparently. To ensure there wasn't a chance anything could be linked back to me, I had to wait a while for my delivery. I paid by postal order so the transaction couldn't be traced back, and arranged for it to be delivered to an old mill at the bottom of town. All I needed to do then was simply turn up on time to meet the postman.

The thing was, when it came to using the stuff, I did exactly as I'd seen on the telly; poured a load of it onto a hanky and clamped it hard around his mouth. But the effect was far from instantaneous. He fought and kicked and jiggled like fuck for what seemed like about five minutes and then, when he finally stopped struggling, it had killed him. I had to resuscitate him – imagine that? Having to bring some poor fucker back to life just so I could kill him again. It was a right pain in the arse. I gave him a couple of aspirin when he came to, to stop his headache, because I wanted him to concentrate fully on the torture I had in mind, and it ended up being a real blessing in disguise as it helped him bleed to death from wounds that would otherwise have just left him seriously scarred.

After the situation with the chloroform, I started looking on the internet to find different ways of knocking people out or poisoning them, and began importing highly dangerous pets; a viper, couple of frogs, a spider. Stuff like that.

It was to house all these out of sight that gave me the kick up the arse to convert the cellar into a proper room; some of these creatures are also very sensitive to changes in temperature, and in a room with no direct sunlight it's a lot easier to regulate this. It was while I was doing it out that I realised that having this private room would give me a safer environment to carry out some of the more complex ideas I'd had, so I soundproofed it as well.

It was during this period of time that I learned to drive, and by the time I'd finished doing up the cellar room I had my license and was desperate to try out something on someone. I was a little too hasty, unfortunately; I made a couple of daft mistakes. They posed no real problem, although at the time it got me a little flustered.

Through research on the internet and various tests on my guinea pig, I found I could create a spray using some of the oily liquid from one of my frogs mixed with water that would knock someone out for a good hour. It took around thirty seconds to work but, when it did, it worked a treat; they just flopped.

I also found out that rat poison works by thickening the blood, and was curious to see if there was a way I could do it undetected by using something a little more creative. So I did my homework. To understand the best way of achieving this objective, I needed to have a solid understanding of how the blood actually clots. Here's what I learned: a blood vessel is basically a pipe that swishes blood from A to B. It's lined with smooth, flat cells called endothelial cells which enable the blood to flow freely. If the pipe breaks, the whole thing fucks up and ruptures so the flowing blood ends up inside. From there, a few things happen: the blood vessel automatically constricts and spasms. This stops the blood from flowing to the damaged area and helps prevent blood loss. Then the exposed pipe attracts circulating platelets, cloudy cells that circulate the body like little security guards ready to assist in clotting just in case. These platelets clump together over the tear in the blood vessel, forming a plug within the first few minutes of the injury. Now, this is all well and good, but the platelets will stay in place unless a substance called fibrin can be made to bind them. There are binding sites on the platelets that attract coagulation proteins, which also spend their time patrolling your insides until they're needed. These coagulation proteins need to be activated in order to produce fibrin, so basically, if you can prevent them from being activated, the blood will simply keep on clotting.

The reason I ended up the with the viper was to use his venom for this purpose. It's one of over a dozen effects that viper venom has on the body, so a controlled amount was needed, enough to cause a rupture and start the clotting, but not so much that the other effects killed the victim. It was a complex problem but I settled on a simple and organic solution. I needed to administer a small amount and then have the blood-clotting aggravated by more natural means.

It was easier than you might think. When someone becomes angry, their heart rate usually increases along with their rate of respiration, so they breathe deeper and harder. Blood pressure rises, the digestive processes are suspended and, as blood is drawn away from the liver, stomach and intestines to flow to the central nervous system and the muscles, the individual's surface temperature rises. Their muscles tense, they become agitated, restless and sometimes hyperactive. All the time this is going on, their blood is going through a natural thickening process. Not enough to kill a person under normal circumstances, but I thought perhaps if they'd had a little shot of viperine venom, some magic might happen.

I couldn't use it on my guinea pig because it would kill him, so I was eager to try it out on some human along with the knock-out spray, but I was kind of clutching at straws when it came to a potential victim. I was a little concerned that there could be a connection established between Uncle Jack and the other guy if it came out that he was a paedo, so I needed someone completely different. The problem was that there wasn't all that much that was newsworthy at that particular time.

I started going to court and just hanging around, watching to see if anyone in the dock deserved it, but ultimately this proved to be a waste of time; they were either found innocent – no good – or sent down. I had a strong inkling that a few of the innocent ones were actually guilty, but without knowing for sure, it didn't really feel right doing it.

John Goodchild ended up as my victim through nothing more than a conversation in a pub. I was in there having a drink with my mate Jonny; he sold me my car and has since then tidily erased any I've had call to send his way. I've known him a long time and knew a lot of his motors came from less than legitimate sources, and he was telling me about how pissed off he was at the bloke who had been cleaning up his cash for him. Jonny categorises things and simple theft, which is his vice, is acceptable in his eyes. What isn't acceptable, however, is cleaning money for more sinister reasons, and it turned out that the guy doing his washing didn't give a flying fuck who he was helping and how it affected people, and in addition wouldn't let Jonny take his business elsewhere, using his army of less than savoury contacts as a threat to retain his business and creep up the fees.

I suppose, in retrospect, my choosing him as a victim could have made things complicated for Jonny. If I'd have been as cautious as I am now, I'd have never picked him because, in delving into his background, the police could have quite easily found out who his clients were and either started to track their activity, or tie them in as a suspect for the murder. Thankfully, the old boys' club that formed the police force at this time was incompetent and found fuck all. Mind you, I suppose someone who launders cash for a living is going to have an intricate and sophisticated means of going about his business and keeping it off the radar, otherwise he'd be fucked anyway.

Even though I made a couple of mistakes on Goodchild, his death is my favourite so far, I think. The sheer planning and organisation of it was far beyond the others, either before it and since. I watched him for a long time and had to do some seriously intricate work to achieve my objective.

His legitimate front was running a small but very exclusive firm of accountants; they were based in the city, a building called The Light, Which is as close to a skyscraper as you can find around Yorkshire, and houses the most prestigious firms in the area. I'd been in there a few times to meet clients as part of my job and after deciding on him as a target, I made a point of snooping around as much as I possibly could whilst I was there. It was a seriously plush place and also a fucking nightmare to find your way around. On my third or fourth snoop, I found Goodchild's office. It was on the eighth floor and at that point I'd pretty much decided that collaring him at work would be nigh on impossible; that was, until a couple of weeks later when I attended a meeting in one of the hired meeting rooms on the first floor.

There are around thirty meeting rooms on that floor with varying levels of facilities (projectors, plasma screens, video conferencing etc.), and of various sizes. Whilst on my way down the long corridor from which they stem, I noticed that on the doors they have a booking schedule saying who has that particular room, and for what time slot they have it booked. I noticed his name appearing twice in a single day on the video conferencing suite. I made a point of going back the following week to see if these were regular scheduled meetings and it appeared that they were.

This provided me with stronger possibilities, being closer to the ground floor, but the situation was still less than perfect. I decided I needed to go for a shit before the hour drive back to Holme Bridge and when I got to the loo, the whole thing started to click into place. When I entered the bathroom on this floor, it was instantly different from the rest, as stationed by the door there was a bloke with various aftershaves, deodorants, mints, hair gel and stuff like that. After all, nobody wants to attend an important meeting not looking or smelling their best, do they?

I heard someone either leave or enter when I was on the shitter, and hurried up to see which it was. Fortunately, it was the prior and I had a good old snoop whilst I was left alone in there. There was a door marked *Private* near the entrance of the loo and I opened it to have a peek inside. It contained some cleaning products and some folded-up linen and a large hatch, but I had no idea what it was for.

I went back into the cubicle and sat waiting to hear the door go, hoping it would be him coming back so I could see what he was up to. After a couple of minutes I heard it and left the cubicle. He had returned with the tablecloth and cushion covers from one of the meeting rooms (probably the one I'd just finished in). As I slowly strolled out, I saw him sling them down the chute and chuckled to myself. It would be perfect. I'd need to do a little more homework, but if I could do his job for a day, spray Goodchild with my knock-out spray, bundle him down the laundry chute and get him at the other end, it'd leave me half an hour to get him into my car, before spraying him again to give me enough time to get him home.

All I had to do was figure out how to get to that bloke's

cleaning/toilet-assisting position and plan a route from wherever the chute spat out, to the car. On my way out, I tried to suss out whereabouts on the ground floor that chute led, and after a little pottering I saw another door marked *Private*. It seemed to be in approximately the same position as the entrance door to the corridor full of meeting rooms on the floor above, and I reckoned it'd be the same set-up. Difference being, if that door was marked *Private,* then the rooms coming off it on this floor were probably the offices of the people responsible for the building itself.

I needed to find a way to get in there and have a nosy, because if I couldn't get to the chute, I wouldn't be able to get to the victim. Over the next few days at work, it became obvious to me that I could get access by going in on a legitimate business appointment. They'd definitely have no use for the packing services my company supply, but they'd have a call for someone to supply cleaning services or temporary staff or something. So I just pretended to be from another company. Fuck me, they were difficult to get in with. I've had some tough sales in my time but getting to speak to the facilities manager in that place was a right bastard. If I'd used as much tenacity getting through to people in my day job, I'd be fucking sales director by now.

I went in and did my best job of bullshitting my way through the appointment. I had been right about the corridor, it housed their security office, sales office, the directors' and managers' offices and a few meeting rooms of their own. Once I'd finished, I had a look around and at the bottom end was a door exactly where the toilets were on the floor above. I walked in and there it was; the tablecloths and seat covers ended up in a large fabric basket about the width of a bath but taller. I peered up the chute just to check that the fall wouldn't kill him on the way down, and it wasn't risk-free. I'd need some luck on my side, in terms of hoping nobody would be wandering around in here, and I'd need to lower him feet first as much of the way as possible, to reduce the chances of him getting seriously injured on the way down. I wasn't too arsed about him breaking a leg or something, but if he broke his neck, it'd ruin what I wanted to try next.

Now, it's worth explaining here that I'm fully aware that this all seems very complicated, and I could easily have got him at home, or followed him where he went drinking and posed as a taxi driver or something, but I wanted to see if I could do it. Nobody improves by playing safe, and I felt that I needed to stretch myself creatively on this one.

So here's what I did. The first thing I needed to do was ensure that the toilet guy and the laundry guy couldn't attend work. This was simple enough. I'd tailed them a couple of times to see where they lived and what they did. The laundry lived on his own and seemed like a bit of a loner, he drank alone in his local boozer most nights. I just spiked his drink with a little light poison, nothing complex, just a little salmonella.

The other guy was little more difficult. Well, morally, anyway. The process was straightforward enough because he had his milk delivered, so all I needed to do was pop a syringe through the foil top and add the salmonella; the moral problem was that of his kids. What could be enough to make an adult ill could be a potentially fatal dose for a child, but I needed to make him ill enough to definitely be off work. I reduced the dosage slightly and just hoped for the best. I think his kids must have been alright because I never saw anything on the local news or in the papers about it. I hope they were, anyway; I don't think I could live with myself if I hurt a child.

So they were both out of action and, as I expected, I got a call on my mobile from the facilities manager of the building asking me for temporary staff. Perfect. All fitted together nicely. I told him that I had nobody available but I'd happily try to cover both jobs.

Once I'd got to work, I needed to ensure that Goodchild needed a shit, so I laced the coffee machine in the video conferencing room with laxatives, not too many, just enough to make him need a shit urgently, and went back to the toilet where I stood and waited.

He rushed past me at some speed and locked himself into a cubicle. The sound and the stench was incredible. I don't know what the fuck that bastard had eaten but Christ the smell of it made me nearly sick. When he came out of the cubicle, I lifted my knock-out spray (which was housed in an eau de toilette bottle) and raised it toward him. He said, "No thanks," but I wasn't going to let that stop me and sprayed the fucker in the face with it, anyway. He started having a go at me and I just smiled as he fell to the floor, clean out cold mid rant, then I dragged him to the cupboard, opened the hatch and lowered him down as slowly and carefully as I could.

Once I got into the laundry room, I realised I'd made a bit of an error because he was lying on the floor with his legs twisted underneath him. Obviously, with the laundry guy not being there, the basket hadn't been placed to catch him, but it was no major problem, it just meant I had to struggle to lift him into it instead.

I bundled the linen on top of him, then wheeled the huge basket into the car park and started mentally preparing for some strenuous work. I had to tip the contents of the linen basket into the boot of my motor without it looking like there was something incredibly heavy in it. I managed okay.

Then I set off home. The thing was, I'd left the spray behind. This wasn't a massive problem as far as Goodchild was concerned; there was plenty more at home. It was, however, a problem that I'd left it in the toilet at The Light. I needed to get him home and get back there as quickly as possible, otherwise there'd potentially be a small mound of passed-out bodies to deal with.

I did as I needed to. He came to just as I was pulling into my street and I was lucky nobody heard him or saw the car shaking, I went straight into the garage, closed the door and got some spray to zap him again before locking him in the cellar, dropping the linen off at the cleaners and getting back to The Light.

I was fortunate in only having one knocked-out body to contend with. I just treated it as if he'd passed out, called the first-aider, and fucked off back home, binning the Sim card for the pay-as-you-go phone number I'd given the facilities manager on the way out.

Once I'd got back, I needed to have a little think; did I go down there and enter what would be a scuffle to get him angry, then jab him with the mixture, or just jab him and hope that got him angry? Each option provided its own risks and merits. The main dilemma was this; taking him on could involve me knocking one of the cages over and us both dying from a bite, but at least there'd be no risk of him dying from the venom's other effects.

I decided to spray him, strip him and wait. I figured the confusion alone should aggravate him. As soon as I saw him coming to, I fired the syringe into him and stood back to watch.

He sat up and started yelling and screaming at me, then he lunged at me, I moved and he yelped. Not in frustration at missing me, but because his blood was starting to thicken and his anger was aggravating it. A shrill, loud scream and he fell to his knees; he was shouting and screaming in agony and begging for help, and pleading and yelling and crying and panicking as the blood slowly thickened in his veins; gasping and spasming and struggling as his heart began to rupture from the pressure, terrified yell after terrified yell as his face changed to a strange shade of pink and the pigment in his cheeks began altering; squirming and panicking as the veins in his head bulged, before screeching and screaming as he collapsed to the floor on his side. He looked up at me before cradling himself and curling into a ball and then the scream stopped. It didn't end. It just stopped; right in the middle, like someone had pressed a mute button on him. It was fucking awesome.

The intense rush that burned through my entire body forced me into a heap on the floor by the side of him, and as I gasped for breath, writhing in ecstasy, I looked at him for ages. He was perfectly mummified, every milligram of terror and pain perfectly captured and preserved. It was the most beautiful thing I've ever seen. I wanted to keep him as an ornament but I couldn't risk it and didn't have the room. Later that night, I bundled him back in the car and dropped him in his own back garden. By now, he had set like stone, so I propped him upright. He looked like a life-size, naked, curled up garden gnome.

Anyway. Now I need to think of a good way to kill this Tim Morris. I could Super Glue his mouth shut and stick his nostrils together. Watch him suffocate or, better still, watch him rip them open before putting him through something else. What if he didn't rip them open, though and just died? It'd a bit wank, really; I'd be more of a spectator... Not my style. Plus, it wouldn't take all that long and I want to really enjoy this one.

I wonder how difficult it would be to attach some sort of thin but strong cabling to him and make him like a human puppet? I could have some fun with him then... No, Jeremy, it's not practical, too complex. Something simple, something straightforward, something agonisingly and excruciatingly painful and slow. Yes, there's no point in rushing the idea; it will make itself apparent when the time is right. For now, I just need to watch him. Understand his regime; know where he's going, when he's going and why he's going. Preparation is the mother of success. This is going to be a good one. I can feel it.

ESCAPING
HOMES AND HOUSES

His memory drifts to staying somewhere with lots of other children, most of whom seem to behave a lot worse than he ever remembered being allowed to. On occasion, people came to have look around, eyeing the children up like someone might eye up a dog in the pound. Sometimes children left and never came back. Sometimes they left and came back really quickly, and others never seemed to go anywhere. He fell into the middle category.

Not that anyone ever asked him about where he'd like to go. He was simply passed from pillar to post, fostered out here and there, sometimes for a few weeks, other times for a few months. There were so many different places that he can barely remember them all; they're in there rattling around somewhere but they don't seem significant enough for him to clarify and store.

He remembers the odd isolated incident, usually bad ones where he was being shouted at for something, or bullied by another child, but they all seem to merge into one clump or category and make little sense.

He remembers the first family in which he got to call someone Mummy. It still upsets him that he remembers her more clearly than his own mother.

76

The Jones family took him in quite soon after he first went into the home. They definitely weren't the first family to take him in, but they were among the first. He remembers at the time thinking how nice it was to be in a proper family. He even had a brother and a sister there, Jacob and Doreen, and they weren't the kind he'd known previously, that were nice to him when people were around and horrible to him once they'd gone away, they were just nice to him all the time. He had around three or four months of what seemed like bliss, and he'd wanted to stay there forever.

Things started to change, though and Mr Jones seemed to be away more and more of the time. Then, when he did come back, there'd be screaming and shouting whilst Doreen, Jacob and he were told to stay upstairs. It was sometimes accompanied by banging and smashing noises, although he never saw what had been damaged or smashed. Mrs Jones wouldn't let them downstairs until everything seemed to be back where it was before.

He noticed her start to change after Mr Jones left with Jacob and Doreen a few weeks later, and realised that she, like his father, seemed to drink a lot more. As the weeks passed, the food in the fridge seemed to deplete and it was replaced by wine. Slowly, the bottle or two of wine she had been drinking a day gave way to five or six larger bottles of strong white cider and Mrs Jones became more and more strange.

He remembers feeling uncomfortable when she held him so tightly and sobbed. As she kissed him before he went to school on a morning, he could smell the stale alcohol, and it was a smell he associated with death, thanks to his father.

On a night, she would insist that he slept with her as she was lonely, and part of him liked the fact that she loved him so much. Another part of him hated her always asking him if he loved her. He told her he did but, at six years old, he didn't know what it meant, he just knew it seemed to make her happy when he told her.

She explained to him one night in a mumbled slur, that if he really loved her he would do something special for her. Something so special that he could never tell anybody because they would be jealous of the love they shared, so he crawled under the sheets and, with his head between her legs, he did as she instructed.

He doesn't remember how long all this went on for, and at the time although he didn't like it, he did have something special and close with someone for the first time in his life. He remembers a lot of confusion when the people from the home came to check up on him, and recalls Mrs Jones begging and pleading with them not to take him away as he was all she had left. He remembers it being explained to him that he had only been allowed to stay there when there was a full family around him, and that because Mr Jones had left with the other children, Mrs Jones wasn't allowed to keep him.

He was back at the home then, and in and out of other people's houses for short spells at a time.

He remembers with great fondness and deep regret one particular family: the Astons; Mary and Andrew and their son, James. He and James became close friends and he stayed with the Astons for over a year. They lived a long way from where he came from and he remembers their accents seeming funny at the time. He noticed that the people around this area seemed friendlier and he enjoyed school a lot more than he ever had previously.

It was also a lot more green than anywhere else he'd been, and after school he would go climbing trees, building dens and constructing 'Tarzan swings' over small streams that James would call 'becks'. They'd take shortcuts home down little alleyways he'd call 'ginnels'. He also remembers wondering why teacakes around there didn't contain any currants.

James introduced him to music. They loved to listen to all his dads' old records and James always let him play with whatever toys he wanted.

They ate meals together at a table every night and even though he'd always been a fussy eater he'd eat everything put on his plate, he remembers this as one of the happiest times of his life and sometimes, on an evening, when he was sure James had drifted off to sleep in the bunk below him, he would say thank you, not to anybody in particular, just because he felt he ought to say it.

James played guitar in the school band and he remembers feeling upset when he had to go away to compete against other schools in competitions, particularly as his dad would accompany him. He felt left out but, as he couldn't play any instruments, he was excluded from the trips. Mary would occasionally take him to watch some of the more local ones and he remembers thinking how nice it was to sit watching with her, like all the other children who had proper mums and dads.

On one of these particular occasions, he remembers seeing James and his dad and congratulating them afterwards. When he asked Mary why they weren't coming back with them, she'd explained that the winners were to play in London, near to where he was originally from, the following day and they couldn't join them as it was too far.

She made him warm milk and jam on toast when they got back, and read him a story until he fell asleep. That night, he dreamt about his father's threat to kill him and although most of the content of the dream has now dissolved, he remembers waking up terrified.

He went to Mary's bedroom to explain that he'd dreamt his dad was trying to kill him, and she'd held him and told him everything would be okay, before drifting back off to sleep. As he'd lain there with his head on her chest, he had never felt such security and contentment, and he'd felt certain that he truly loved somebody for the first time ever. He expressed that love in the only way he'd been taught how, by Mrs Jones, and couldn't understand why Mary started screaming and shouting at him and calling him disgusting.

He was back in the home again the day after, and spent a lot of time locked in a room being asked questions and told to draw pictures. It was during this period that they explained to him that what Mrs Jones had asked him to do was a very bad thing, although they didn't say exactly why.

After a long period of time without being taken in by another family, he began to feel rejected; he couldn't understand why nobody wanted him and sometimes this made him feel actual physical pain, as well as emotional – a deep, twisting ache just below his chest and above his stomach. He cried himself to sleep for nights on end, until he realised that there was no point in crying anymore.

This was a defining moment in his life, and once he'd made this realisation, he vowed never to cry again. Instead, he looked at his problem, quickly thought it through to its solution, and made the decision that he needed to reach that solution by any means necessary.

Almost overnight, he changed. He began helping the staff in the home. He didn't argue with the other children any more. Instead, he listened to them and empathised, never once wanting the returned favour of a friendly ear. Whenever visitors came, he was the perfect child, polite, well-behaved and amusing. It didn't take him long to get placed and he kept up the charade all the time, having found that if you please everyone, life ends up easier.

His life had changed; he'd learned the art of manipulation. Now, all he needed to do was perfect his craft.

JUSTICE
REALISATION

I'm on holiday, I think it's Spain. Maybe Greece. Definitely Europe. The hotel is quiet and clean and I'm there with a friend. We're ready to go out on the town and we meet two girls at the bar who are talking to two guys; one of the guys is long and thin, and the other's short and fat. On closer inspection, it seems that only one of the girls is talking whilst the other one stares vacantly into space. We get a drink and head over to introduce ourselves to the four of them. I can't make out their names, but the quiet girl catches my attention. She is still ignoring everyone and everything else going on around her, and isn't forthcoming with any conversation of any kind, but she's making eye contact with me and smiling.

I look a little closer and realise that it's her. Facially, she looks exactly the same but she's put on some weight. It's definitely her, though. Strangely, although in conventional terms she's less attractive than she would usually appear, the fact that she looks so different attracts me even more. There's a real sense of the unknown as to what her body will look like once I manage to remove her clothing – *if* I manage.

Her friend announces that they have to leave as they have tickets for some club. When they leave, her friend says goodbye to everyone and kisses them on the cheek. She, however, says one single goodbye. The rest of the guys assume it's directed at all of us, but her eyes met mine so I know it was exclusively for me.

I try to find out what club they're going to, and the two guys that had been talking to them encourage us not to bother going to find them. They tell us that we've no chance... That they've been there all week and although the long guy looks like he's got a chance with the chatty bird, the deal won't get closed unless the frosty bird finds someone. I tell them that I can thaw out the frosty one and tell the long man not to worry. My friend and the wide man decide they don't fancy going; the club they've gone to plays predominantly trance music and they want to listen to funky house.

The long man and I head out into the streets to look for this club, some guy giving out flyers offers to walk us there, and then we're inside. The club is huge, like a large strobe-lit village full of identical pill-heads. It shouldn't be too difficult to spot them in here. Everyone is exactly the same. Then, twinkling in the distance like a star, I see her – she's too far away to make out, but I'd bet that the glimmering is lights reflecting off her silky, shiny, silver dress.

I grab Long Man by the arm and we charge through the clone crowd. As we get nearer, I can see that I was correct; it is her. She's using her elbow to prop herself up on a table while her friend dances. I approach her and ask her if she wants to dance, but she explains that she thinks she may have been spiked or had too much to drink, because she feels dizzy and can't walk properly. Long Man goes to speak to her mate and we offer to walk them home.

They agree. Long Man charges off with the chatty bird and I'm left trailing with her friend. I put her arm around my shoulder and put my arm around her waist to help her walk. Suddenly, we're back outside and, as we walk, I can see that whilst I've been struggling to walk with her and hold her up, the hand I had around her waist has ended up securing her around the ribs and, in the process, has lifted her skirt three or four inches. As I glance down, I notice that every now and then it goes a little higher than it should, considering she's clearly not wearing any underwear. I don't want her to be exposed to everyone, and neither do I want her thinking I'm grabbing sly, perving glances, so I let go for a moment, allowing the skirt to fall back down before gripping her again, this time on her hip. If she was wearing underwear, I'd be able to feel it through the flimsy dress, but all I can feel is her soft, plump, flesh. The silk clings to her so well that, to the touch, she may as well be naked.

We're back in the girl's hotel room and she starts kissing me. I stop her because I don't want to take advantage, but she assures me that she's fine again now and kisses me again. Long Man sits watching us whilst chatty bird is on the loo. He sticks a thumb up before heading towards the bathroom to join her.

I kiss her and it's marvellous. I grasp at her breasts and they're bigger and squishier than normal. I like it. She's kneeling down and with my other hand I start to softly, slowly, work my way up from the knee to rub her. But once I get there, I'm disappointed to find that she's really dry and I begin to feel concerned that I don't turn her on. I move my hand away slowly and she says her parents' place isn't far from here and then we're walking through their front door. There's some woman sat knitting in the corner in a floral rocking chair, there's a door next to her and a table next to the door with an odd-looking lizard on it. It has a friendly, smiley face but I can see intent in its eyes. It scares me. The woman in the rocking chair looks up and says hello and by the time I finish introducing myself, I realise that my silky clad girl has gone through the door next to her. I head towards it and pause, as the little lizard on the table looks to be sizing me up. I rationalise; she walked past it and through the door without any problems, so I should be fine. I move quickly and as I go past, the lizard puffs out into a porcupine-like ball of spikes and scratches my arm as I slip through the door.

Once in there, we're in a bathroom rather than a bedroom and she's brushing her teeth, I look around the bathroom; it's a normal, simple affair, clean and tidy with a fallen cactus in a pot on the window ledge. But, on closer inspection, I can see that the cactus is actually a small, spiky man who seems to be having trouble getting up.

Now it's the day after and we're all in the bar area again. The girls are dressed as cheerleaders, yellow outfits with a blue trim. Once again, they have club tickets. I wave goodbye and she beckons me to follow. I sprint out of the bar area after her and towards the pool she's walking alongside, and she grabs me by the hand and pulls me through a door marked *Private*. There's a long corridor and she races down it before dragging me through another door into a closet filled with cleaning products. At the back, there's another door. This one's only waist height and we have to crawl through it on our hands and knees. Once we're in there, she kicks the door shut, sits on something resembling a small boiler, and removes her top. Her large, imperfect breasts impress me and I kiss them before hearing a fire alarm or something.

Typical! The fucking sleep alarm. Am I going mad? Why should I be here, lying in bed with aching balls, feeling frustrated about a girl that doesn't even exist outside my own unconscious mind?

I need a fucking drink, but it's not worth it. I've got an appointment in an hour or so with Tim Morris. I feel I need to let him know that I'm working with Julie and explain why. He won't be happy, but ultimately my reasons for getting her involved are honourable ones. I also want to warn him that I fear he may be a target now for the killer. That article has left him wide open and he definitely fits the bill as someone local who would have a string of suspects from here to China. Whilst I'm there, I need to get some clarification on the points raised in that article, too; I truly can't see that he can be responsible for such horrific dealings, but nothing is beyond the realms of possibility, I suppose. I hope I'm right, I hope he didn't do anything wrong, so I can explain everything to Julie and she can print a retraction. It could save his life.

*

Just looking at his door fills me with fear and dread. He's going to be so fucking angry with me. He'll probably hit me. What if he does? I'll just have to take it, I suppose, dust myself off, remain calm and reassure him. My training is still fresh enough to talk anyone around and get information from even the most terrifying and guarded of people, but I'm in control of those situations. I can plan the course of my argument and execute it to perfection, but here, I'm at a loss. The nerves are clouding my judgement, and the fact that I actually really like the guy throws a huge spanner in the works.

Knock, just knock on the door, you fucking pussy. Rip the plaster off. Get it over with. Okay, here goes – a deep breath and… There. I regain my composure, there's no sense in looking coy when he opens the door. I can hear someone moving inside and as the sounds grow louder, I steady my nerves and brace myself for the opening of the door. But it doesn't come.

"Who is it?" he shouts.

"It's me, Scott. Come to see how you are and talk over a few things." I can hear him either moving or moving things.

"Hang on then."

I hear him move towards the door, then away again, and he comes back. He puts the keys into the lock, I hear it turn and as quick as a flash the door opens and he drags me inside the house, slamming it behind me.

"Was there anyone out there?" he asks, twitchy. He looks panicked, pretty worse for wear, too, in all honesty. About four or five days' growth of stubble around his chin and, by the smell of him, I reckon that when he last had a shave was also when he last had a wash. He's wearing a blue dressing gown and even though I'm only in the hallway, the house smells like the tap room of a 1920's boozer. Like he's done nothing but chain smoke and get pissed out of his face since the suspension.

"Well?" he asks.

"Sorry?"

"Was there anybody out there?" he says again, darting his head left and right.

"Oh… No. No I don't think so."

He grabs my shoulders and squeezes them hard. "What do you mean, you don't think so? Was there or wasn't there?"

I lift an eyebrow and half smile, nodding as if to tell him to chill the fuck out. "Not to my knowledge, Tim, no." I loosely grab his arms and release them from my shoulders. "But to be honest, I wasn't actually taking any notice, mate. What are you going on about?"

He leads me into his living room, which, as I already suspected, is littered with empty cans. There are a couple of ashtrays on a table strewn with newspaper pages that are so full, the ash in them is spilling over the sides. He swipes at the base cushion of a chair that's covered in crumbs and possibly peanuts and tells me to sit down.

"I'm being watched," he says. He sits on the sofa against the back wall to my right and leans forward towards me. "I don't know who. National press, maybe, someone with a grudge, or internal affairs."

I need to clarify whether he's actually in some sort of paranoid delusion or if his concerns are genuine. I know it's obvious internal affairs will be watching him like a hawk, but they're too good to let him know about it outwardly. They'll have tapped his phone, be monitoring his p.c. and screening his mail, but Tim will know this as well as I do. I decide to tell him, anyway.

"Internal affairs are bound to be watching you mate."

"Yeah, yeah I know. Probably the press, too. Fucking scum wankers, they don't give a flying fuck about anything but getting themselves a fucking story. Glory hungry vermin. That's all they are. They don't do anything in the best interests of the public, they just fuck people over to get some cash. Christ! They even build people up purely to fuck them over and get some cash. They disgust me."

Well, I wasn't expecting that. "If the press are after you, there's fuck all you can do about it. You'll just have to grit your teeth and get on with everything. Being holed up in here getting shitfaced every day will only add weight to a story, if they decide to run one." Here comes my killer closed question. I'll know for definite whether he did it or not, regardless of the answer. "Plus, you've got nothing to hide. That stuff that was in the *Gazette* was all bollocks, right?"

Fuck me, he did it. He hasn't even answered yet and I know for a fucking fact that he did it. There's a pause – a split second pause when someone's done something wrong; that split second is their brain looking up possible answers to the question like it's flicking through a roller deck filled with bullshit. If he hadn't done it, I'd have been shouted at already, instantly.

Here we go, he speaks... Will it be bullshit? "I've been in the police force for almost thirty years. You can't even begin to comprehend some of the things I've seen, heard and had to deal with in that time." He's flopped back in his chair and he's taking a gulp of lager. "This world is vile," he says, "vile, disgusting, cruel and corrupt to its core. Even here in Holme Bridge. People blissfully looking around seeing the trees, greenery, old cottages and the Pennines on the horizon, but all I can see is scum. Eating the planet like a cancer and it needed dealing with. I can't do everything; I'm just one man. But I couldn't sit back and watch whilst our village imploded. Do you know how many paedophiles there are on the sex offenders register in this village?"

I'm a little too shocked to add much to the conversation at this point. "Erm... No," I reply

"Twenty-seven." He uses the syllables to make a point, it takes almost thirty seconds to say just those two words and, to be honest, I'm surprised by this amount and am about to speak when he pipes up again. "Just in this area, I mean – obviously they're not all a serious threat. Some of them were looking at professionally produced foreign glossy porn involving girls of sixteen or seventeen that's legal in the country it was made, but others are most certainly not. Others are sexual predators that are a severe danger to every child in our village. Something needed to be done, Scott. I know my solution was a little unorthodox, but I did what I needed to do to protect our community. A community let down by a fucking prison service that allows depraved perverts like those to roam the streets. And the human rights campaigners, shit! They're the fucking biggest bastards of them all. Constantly giving these people the ammunition to contest and convince people they can be, or have been, rehabilitated. Paedophiles should be fucking culled!"

What a fucking bell end. "So you thought that the best thing to do would be to sell children to them?" I can't believe my ears and I feel queasy.

"Look. I was declaring war on the crime virus infecting this vicinity, and in any war there's going to be collateral damage. My solution wasn't ideal but it was definitely effective. Since my operation got into full flow, there's been no missing children or reports of sexual abuse to a minor."

"But what about the kids whose lives you ruined?"

"I feel bad for them. I do. But ultimately, their parents were willing to sell them as slaves to make a better life for the rest of their families. The money they get is enough to buy a house and start up a business where they're from. It sets them up for generations to come. At the end of the day, those kids' lives were ruined, anyway. They were living in poverty, hand to mouth, and would have died from infection or starvation sooner or later."

"You mean their parents actually knew what they were being sold for?"

"Fuck, yeah. All that promise of a better life bollocks in the *Gazette* was a pile of old shit. They weren't lured, they were bought. And their parents knew exactly what for and exactly why."

I feel sick. "Who could fucking sell a child? How could any parent do that?"

"It happens. Truly, it happens a lot in the east, families sell off their oldest son so that he can be tortured and killed by businessmen on a power trip, in return for enough money to change their future. Like I said – the world is a corrupt place."

"But they were just kids, Tim."

"I know. And there isn't a day goes past that I can clear my head of that. That's why I fucking drink so much. It doesn't help me forget, but it does numb the ache of the guilt."

I can't believe that all this time I never noticed he was alcoholic. He was bloody good at hiding it. A sort of functional junkie, I suppose. Which brings me on to my next point.

"So what about the drugs, then?"

He takes a deep breath and sparks himself up a cigarette. "Scott, I want you to know from the offset that none of this is about money. It's all purely about what's best for this village."

"Okay."

"Drugs are the main reason for most other crime. It's like the top of the pyramid. It filters down from there; you've got people needing a hit, people not paying what they owe. Those people are theft. I'd bet my last penny that over ninety percent of petty robberies, burglaries and car theft in this country is down to drugs one way or another. Also, drug dealers hook people in. They take vulnerable people, give them a few free hits and before you know it, bang! Their whole life's down the shitter. To be perfectly honest, I couldn't give a shit about weed and pills, or coke to a certain extent. Stoners and pill-heads pose no real threat to our community for the most part. Most of them are just weekenders letting off steam – not all of them, of course, but it's definitely a minority. Crack and heroin is where the problem lies for the most part, so it was those I started with. I knew that if I could get control over the supply with a network of dealers abiding by strict rules, I could cut the crime and hopefully slowly wean people off."

"Wean people off?"

"Yeah, each case is dealt with on an individual basis. I pretty much managed to stop crack happening before it even started around here. In most areas, it ends up infecting a community when the fucking Yardies storm into an area, as they'll bully out the heroin dealers and offer a free rock of crack with every hit of brown. Before you know it, they've doubled their money and doubled the crime in the area to fund it. Plus, people chasing cash for crack are more volatile than people chasing for heroin. More likely to perform violent crimes like muggings. I got a hold of the heroin situation just before those Yardie cunts tried to muscle in. The heroin I supply is clean, and cut with clean materials. With every hit supplied to an individual, the percentage of the core drug is slightly decreased, in fact there are some people in this area on less than a third of the standard dose. And the regularity at which they're buying is decreasing considerably. Plus, my dealers know that they have complete immunity as long as they stick to the rules, which basically means that they deal – they don't push."

He takes another swig of his drink and drag of his fag, then smirks. A smug expression fades onto his dishevelled face and I don't know what to do. Tim's clearly absolutely fucking deluded, he's obviously not going to lie about it when it comes to his hearing. He thinks he's some kind of fucking saviour. It's time for some home truths.

"You really think that what you were doing is a good thing?"

"Of course. Why else would I have done it? How else do you think our crime rate dropped so considerably? I got done what needed to be done."

"Tim, they're going to throw the fucking book at you, man. You're a fucking kingpin drug dealer and you're in the slave trade. Are you insane?"

He tries to justify everything again but I cut him off. "Tim! You're a drug dealer! You sell fucking kids to paedos! Just listen to that. There's no justifying what you're doing. Shit, I bet every criminal on the face of this planet has some reason for doing what they do, but yours is no better or worse. You're fucking sick. And I don't mean sick as in the sick and twisted sense – although you are that also. I mean sick as in ill. Not well. If you could hear yourself in an interrogation room, you'd be appalled. I can't stay here and listen to this, Tim. You've caused more damage to the credibility of the police force than the rest of the fuckers you've been going on about put together! Do you know what I'm having to do to repair the fucking shower of shite you've rained down on us? I'll tell you, I'm having to partner up with Julie Newton, the lass that wrote that article, to hopefully show her that we're not all corrupt, and that we can be trusted to look after our community in an ethical and proper way. You're a fucking prick!"

I stand up and head for the door, but he jumps to his feet and drags me back, throws me in the chair and yells in my face.

"You don't know what I've seen, what I know! Someone needed to do something!"

"It's not up to you to play God, Tim!"

He breaks down in tears as he kneels before me, then he looks up and through his snivels he manages, "I took a statement from an eleven-year-old girl who described in detail the fucking depths of depravity that her mother's addiction to heroin had dragged her to. Her mother needed a hit so badly, she traded her daughter's arse to the fucking dealer! Her eleven-year-old daughter's arse for a fucking hit. Not only that, she was there whilst he raped her – holding her hand! She even injected the eleven-year-old with some heroin so she wouldn't feel the pain! Someone needed to do something!"

"We *all* need to do something, Tim."

I leave him weeping on the floor and go. I'm still at a loss as to what to do. I should report him straight away, tell the boss that he admitted everything, but prison would be too good for him. I'm going to leave it. He can tell them himself at the hearing – if he makes it that far. Hopefully, my instincts will be right and my serial killer will get to him first.

PSYCHOTIC
MORE TO LIFE

I'm well into my thirties now and what I have to show for my life seems so insignificant sometimes. It's seven years since my first kill and I think, after this next one I'll tie up the loose ends in my long-term project and it'll be time to hang up my hat. I'm not saying I'll never kill again, in much the same way as every now and then I'll still do the odd line, or smoke the odd cigarette when I'm pissed, even though I don't actively do either anymore. Plus, by saying you're never going to do something again you're setting yourself an unrealistic target.

I know it's been seven years since the first one because I went to my nephew's seventh birthday party the other day. A load of his annoying little mates running around my sister's house, fucking around on the bouncy castle and stuff she'd hired and put up in the garden, really got me to thinking. All the kids' mums and dads were there and as you'd expect, most of them were sat around getting pissed and talking about 'family' shit. Holidays, outings, christenings, confirmations, yada, yada, yada. But it made me realise that the most important thing in this life is creating more life. Otherwise, what the fuck is the point in being here in the first place? I look at my nephew and I just love him so much, but that's nothing compared to the love he has in his eyes when he looks at his own mother. Same with the rest of those kids and their parents.

I can't even hold down a steady relationship – well, I couldn't even if I wanted to; not with my pastime. So I'm thinking now that maybe it's about time to do something about it. I had a relationship once and it hurt so much when it ended that part of me is terrified of getting so close to someone again, but I'm going to have to.

What will I do about the urge to kill, though? It's not like they have self-help groups for people like me – "Hello, my name's Jeremy Wilkinson and I'm a serial killer" and all that bollocks. I've got no option but to go it alone.

I think if I make this next one really good it'll take the edge off. You know, do the best possible job I can do and know in my heart of hearts that, as much as I try I can never, ever better it. That should help. It's going to be difficult, though; he's being watched like a hawk. I think his house is under surveillance. It's been difficult to figure out the best way of doing it. He has everything delivered and rarely goes out. Short of nicking a fucking Tesco van and pretending to be delivering his shopping, I don't really know what to do. Even then, I can't stay in the house for long enough without rousing some suspicion. What I've got in mind for him is so fucking good though. I can't wait. I'll come up with a way of getting him out and about.

So anyway, I've already started making some preparations for my new life once I'm done with him. I've flogged the pets, all but the guinea pig. I didn't want to just kill them, although that would have been a very easy solution, so I contacted the people I originally bought them from and sold them back. For a lot less than I paid for them, too but at least I knew they'd be going to a good home. I bought a gun with the money, I've never shot anyone before and I plan to put that right before I call it a day. I don't fancy killing Tim Morris with a bullet, it'll be too good for him, but I'll definitely unload into him to see what it's like. I'm going to save my kill until bonfire night, too, just so nobody will think twice if they hear the shots being fired.

I'm in the middle of redecorating down in the cellar at the moment. The room is a lot bigger than it looks. I reckon I can put a little self-contained bedsit down there. Or a really good sized bedroom with a nice en-suite, maybe.

As I'm browsing through the Ikea catalogue and flicking my fingers across its smooth glossy pages, I'm reminded of my last kill. It was a really good one; a well-chosen subject, a well-planned and executed torture process and a good, solid kill. It wasn't my most enjoyable, but it was definitely my best organized and implemented. A friend of mine called Rizwan had been getting a lot of shit from a group of lads he knew for being 'too westernised'. He told me all about it and it turned out that there was a preacher called Akbar Aslam who had been doing a number on a few disillusioned and impressionable minds. One of Rizwan's nephews had come home and wouldn't drink Coca Cola any more because he said it was made by Jews.

I asked Rizwan if I could borrow a copy of the Koran. He wanted to know why, for obvious reasons, so I explained to him that I was brought up a Catholic and I was just curious about its content. You're conditioned to feel heavy guilt for everything when you're brought up a Catholic. It makes you paranoid. I stopped going to church when I reached high school and had the choice, and managed to stay away from one until my sister got married when I was eighteen. When we went into the church, the first thing on the agenda was a hymn. I'd sung the hymn many times at primary and middle school but never really cared about the words and as I read them, I began to feel physically sick – *All that I am, all that I do, all that I'll ever have I offer now to you*. I remember thinking, fucking hell Catholicism is just one massive cult. Throughout the readings, the responses were littered with stuff like "Lord, I am not worthy to receive you". I almost had a fucking panic attack. I've been to church twice since and both times it's nearly resulted in me going mad and storming out.

Uncle Jack's funeral was a fucking classic. The priest went on for about fifteen minutes about how much Uncle Jack had suffered, before saying, 'But I know someone else who suffered… JESUS! Jesus suffered! Jesus suffered so that all of us could be here today."

Now, for obvious reasons I didn't really give a flying fuck that this ruined Uncle Jack's funeral, but it just showed that even when people are at their most upset and vulnerable, the Catholic church won't miss an opportunity to throw Jesus into the fucking mix.

Then, I had to be present at my nephew's baptism. I tried to convince my sister not to get him baptised and told her how I felt about going into a church, but she convinced me, saying that she was only getting him baptised so that he could go to the Catholic school where the grades were better and there was less fighting. She promised me that she'd tell him to ignore all the religious mumbo jumbo once he was old enough, and said that I had to go because I going to be his godfather. Anyway, I went – and surprise, surprise, they used it as another fucking opportunity to ramble on about fucking Jesus.

It was around this time that I began to start reading up on most of the major religions, and a few of the minor ones, too. I wanted to see for myself what all the fuss was all about, and see if I could figure out which one was right. Religion is responsible for most of what's wrong in the world, in my opinion. It makes my fucking blood boil! Wars, fucking crime, famine, hunger, terrorism, murder and fuck knows what else, all for something some bastard, or bastards, wrote down in a fucking book years ago. Have they ever stopped to think that just maybe, just perhaps, there's a slight fucking chance that the people who wrote these books were wrong? Is that so beyond the realms of fucking possibility? Jesus! Have these people not seen *Planet of the fucking Apes*?

I mean, think about it, that's all I'm saying. Jews, Catholics, Buddhists, Islamics, Sikhs, Baptists and Tom Cruise can't all be fucking right, can they? So someone, somewhere is wrong. That's a fact. That's a cold, hard fact and, regardless of who you are and what you believe, you'll never be able to argue with that. Oh, and they'll no doubt argue that it's the others that are all wrong and it's theirs that's the right one. Well, how the fuck do they know? The only thing that fucking book they cling onto like some security blanket proves, is that some fucker wrote a book.

I asked a priest when I was younger. I asked him, "How do you know?" And do you know what his answer was? "Faith." Well, you can take your faith and shove it right up your fucking arse, thank you very much. Faith doesn't get suicide bombers and wankers that crash planes into buildings very far, does it?

I asked my mate Rizwan what the appeal was for these young kids. How could they be possibly convinced that what they were told to do would benefit anyone, anywhere? He told me that they're told that, as they'll be martyrs, they'll sit at the right hand of Allah, they'll drink the finest wines (bear in mind it's against their religion to drink here in real life) and they'll have their pick of the finest virgins.

Now, as nice as that sounds – and it does sound nice – I think these suicide killers have been forgetting to ask one simple question before they go off and fucking blow themselves to smithereens, taking out anyone in a one hundred yard radius. It's a simple question. I'm putting myself in their shoes when the mission's given out now, and the question just rolls out of my mouth. If I had some bearded old cunt telling me to crash a plane into a building for a reward of wine and virgins and to be sat at the right hand of God, I'd say, "Hang on a minute. Hang on just one fucking minute! If it's so good, and everything you've just told me is one hundred percent true, why don't you just do it yourself?" Because I'll tell you what, if I was privy to such information and knew there was a guaranteed spot up there where I could get pissed hangover-free for eternity and fuck fit, V.D.-free birds all day without having to worry about pregnancies, work, mortgage and bills, I wouldn't be telling anyone.

So anyway, I borrowed Rizwan's Koran and read it, and I'll be honest, it made a lot of sense. They basically worship God (Allah), not Jesus, and the moral code running throughout the book is very strong. It is, in fact, not too dissimilar to what Jesus was trying to preach when he was around. His was like a cross between Islam and Buddhism with more boozing (it's only once he'd fucking died that people stopped listening properly to what it was he had had to say, and started just worshipping him instead).

The thing in the Koran that grabbed my attention in particular was section 109, simply entitled, *The Disbelievers*. Here it is, word for word: *In the name of Allah, the Beneficent, the Merciful: Say: Oh unbelievers! I do not serve that which you serve, nor do you serve Him Whom I serve: Nor am I going to serve that which you serve, nor are you going to serve Him Whom I serve: You shall have your religion and I shall have my religion.*

Now, to me, that pretty much says – live and let live. That's from the book that these hate preachers use, for fuck's sake! That one passage says the opposite of what these wankers say to brainwash young lads! So I wanted to find out from the horse's mouth exactly what his opinion would be on that passage before I made him a fucking martyr – except the way that I'd planned it, nobody would ever think of him as a martyr.

He was a lot tougher to get alone than I had originally anticipated. Safety in numbers, I suppose, and he was and still is, my most risky kill in terms of my own personal safety. The police were a walk in the park compared to what his little minions would do to me if they ever found out. I couldn't get him in the mosque, not because he wasn't alone in there, you understand. He was probably alone in there more than anywhere else, it's just that old matter of respect. I mean, I hate religion – I fucking despise it with a passion – but it makes me sick when I see reports on the news of churches, mosques, Buddhist monasteries and suchlike being defiled. People need hope, otherwise all that's left is despair and I didn't want to be responsible for feeding despair. I also didn't want this to turn into a race issue, because I despise racism, too. This one had to be handled particularly carefully to make sure that, rather than creating some kind of backlash within the community, it provided a sense of awakening and understanding.

I couldn't get him at home because there were simply so many people living in his house that there'd be far too many witnesses. I needed a ruse to get him to me. I found out from Rizwan that this guy had a website so I had a look at it. It was nothing too spectacular, just a series of forums where people exchanged quips about how westerners are fucking wankers, and stuff like that. These fuckers are seriously racist. I don't know how they get away with it. As I said, I'm not racist at all but you can bet your knackers that if I registered www.paki-bastards.com, it'd take about two fucking minutes for the police to show up and arrest me, but somehow these twats can do what they want. I decided to log in and join a discussion group, I popped in a little nugget of untrue information about me developing a virus from the toxins of my illegal pets. I used an untraceable Hotmail account as my contact details and made sure that all my correspondence was done from internet cafés. It didn't take long before he contacted me to find out more details. Perfect. I had him.

I arranged a meet, told him to come alone. I said I'd meet him in a lay-by three quarters of the way up the Saddleworth road, that leads to the M62 between Oldham and Halifax. It's deserted up there, all bar a few doggers, and I knew that if I saw the car pull up and he wasn't alone, I could simply drive away. I was super careful. I mean, I always am, but more so with this one. I changed the plates on the car, got into the lay-by and did a three point turn so that I was facing out, ready to go, just in case. As it turned out, I was right to be cautious because he turned up in a Honda Civic that had at least five passengers. I was pretty concerned at this point; there was no way I could burn off that Honda Civic if they decided to give chase. My car was faster than it, but not by a lot. So I waited; I waited and watched as he exited the Honda and approached my driver's side window, and as he started to bend down to peer through, I screeched away and joined the motorway, knowing that by the time they could catch me up, I'd already be a half junction closer to Manchester, or half a junction closer to home. It wouldn't be worth them bothering.

After this, I contacted him by email the following day telling him that I didn't trust him and that the deal was off. The tone of his emails seemed to immediately soften at this stage. I had him where I wanted him. I imagined that if he got a sniff of a virus for sale, he wouldn't be able to keep it to himself. He'd have to feed it up the food chain and I reckoned that by now, he'd have to get his hands on it or risk losing some respect from the people that mattered. Now I could call the shots. He was mine.

I told him that because he had gone back on his word last time, I had lost trust in him. Told him we'd meet in the same place and that once there, he was to leave his car and get into my passenger seat. And here's the best bit; I told him he had to wear cycling shorts and a short T-Shirt, so that he had no way of concealing a weapon. Practical and funny.

He did as I'd told him, and once he was in the car I suggested he call off anyone that he had instructed to follow us, and then give me his phone. He argued for a bit at first, but eventually he did it. He had some serious trust issues, I'm telling you. And rightly so, considering that he wasn't far off being tortured and sliced open.

I made small talk with him for several minutes before blasting him with some knock-out spray, I didn't really need to, but I couldn't be fucking arsed speaking to him, to be honest. A nice little blast would keep him out until I got him into my cellar.

Once there, I stripped him and shackled him to the bed, face up by his chest and feet, made myself a nice cup of tea and waited for him to come round. As I sat, I pondered. After watching the marvellous effect of the blood-thickening agent I'd designed in my previous kill, I'd already decided I was going to use it again. I was going to enjoy torturing him for a while first, though, though I wished I had something that would involve a large amount of excruciating pain but left no physical traces. I remember wishing that I could devise a concoction that was a syringe full of pure pain. Absolute disgusting, agonising anguish lasting just long enough for someone to survive it unscathed. No such luck, unfortunately; I would have to do things the old-fashioned way.

I wanted something that would drive him insane without leaving any bruising or scaring, and decided on sleep deprivation. It was a pretty simple process – although it would need a little baby-sitting at the front end. The method I chose to adopt was pretty crude but definitely effective. I had one of those crappy Gymbody machines that was supposed to help you build a six-pack. It's one of those things where you pop pads on your flabby bits and small electric currents pulse through to work the muscles. I had a fiddle around with it, removed the pads and realised I could easily just tape the wires to the skin, which livened up the jolt a fair old amount. Then I removed the limiter from the base unit to make the pulse stronger. I bought a small portable ECG machine from E-Bay and all I needed to do then was set them up to the laptop and have the Gymbody kick into gear when his heart-rate dropped. It would take baby-sitting because I didn't know how much of a jolt I'd need to wake him, or how far his heart-rate would need to drop to trigger it.

I connected the ECG pads to his chest so that he couldn't wriggle them off and taped the wires of the Gymbody to his temples, nipples and scrotum, then finished my tea whilst I waited for him to come round. His heart-rate was a steady thirty-seven but it shot up when he came to.

He went fucking nuts! Shouting and screaming at me in fucking Punjabi! Spitting everywhere, too. I fucking damn near pissed my pants laughing. Once he'd calmed down a little, he started to make a bit more sense, and glared at me, "You fucking idiot!" he yelled, wide-eyed and manic. "You've just put a nail in your own coffin."

I laughed and sarcastically giggled, "'Course I have, you fucking bell-end. That's why I'm the one strapped to a bed with my bollocks wired up to the mains."

He screamed something about Allah and told me I was going to die.

"Yes, that's right," I said, "I'm definitely going to die, but that'll probably be many years from now, after I've spent some time dribbling into my lap in an old people's home with my brain fucked from all the drugs I did in my younger years."

He started rambling again so I gave him a little jolt. He did a camp little shriek. It was so funny that I jolted him a couple more times for good measure and my own amusement. I asked him if he was hungry and he told me to get fucked, which I thought was a little bit rude.

I pursued my questing regarding his justification for his hatred towards the west, and had to shock him many times before he was forthcoming with the information. It turned out that the Koran I'd read was pretty watered down, even the spelling. It should have been Qu'ran. I'll be honest, the conversation I had with him was pretty interesting once he calmed down. Interesting, but still pointless. The fact was that for every passage he gave me that incited hatred and violence, there were another two that suggested people be left alone. He told me that if he can't convert by the mouth, he is bound to convert by the sword. I told him that suicide attackers didn't use swords and that they never tried to convert anyone by the mouth before storming in and killing people, but he didn't seem to grasp what I was saying. I was trying to get across to him that if he wanted to take a book so literally in terms of its suggestions, then he should take it literally in its entirety.

I pushed him on the fact that the book claims that the sun sets into the sea, something which is one hundred percent proven to be wrong, and challenged the fact that if it were wrong, surely it's possible there could be plenty of other inaccuracies.

Once my interest dropped, I became frustrated with his argument. It was weak, a weak, thin, pathetic argument void of any cold, hard facts, and whenever I came back with a passage that promoted free love and free will, he came back with one that said Jews and Christians should be killed.

So after a while I sat and waited... And waited... And waited until he nodded off, then I checked his heart-rate, set my contraption to shock, giggled when he jolted and yelled at me, and left, closing the door behind me.

I left him two days and when I returned, he looked fucked. I didn't want him to die of starvation or dehydration so I offered him water and food. Nothing spectacular, just nourishment shakes. He objected for a while, but by the time the evening rolled around, he caved in. I sat down on the bed next to him and cradled his head as I helped him drink the water and the shakes. He fucking reeked of piss, shit and sweat, but I was fucked if I was cleaning him as well as feeding him. I think he misunderstood my intentions as I fed him and he started to try and appeal to my better nature. He told me if I let him go now, everything would be fine and he wouldn't tell anyone. I calmly explained that it wasn't time to let him go yet and told him I'd be back again in two more days to feed him again.

When I returned, he looked awful and smelled even worse, his lips had chapped and gone a blue colour, he was shivering and when he spoke, he sounded drunk. I fed and watered him again and this perked him up, but as soon as the first pint of water went into his system, I realised he wasn't shivering at all; he was sobbing, uncontrollably sobbing. He must have cried so much that he'd dehydrated himself and his body simply couldn't produce any more tears. This time his pleading changed. He didn't want to be set free any more, he wanted to die. I told him it wasn't time yet and left him again.

I returned daily to feed him, but his body seemed to have a huge capacity for burning up the food. Perhaps it was due to the fact he wasn't having any sleep and his body was having to use more fuel. I don't know.

After eight days of no sleep and pretty much constant electric shocks he was hallucinating, his yelling and screaming had become more random and he was clinging onto reality, and probably life, with his fingertips. If I left him much longer, he'd die for sure. It was time. I told him, I said, "It's time to end it." He thanked me, it was strange. This guy actually looked relieved that he was going to die. The first time in days, he'd seemed happy.

I gave him a shot of the coagulant. Not as much as I'd used before, because I wanted to keep him alive whilst I carried out my work.

I secured him more firmly to the bed by pulling the luggage strap tighter around the top of his chest, then put a second one around his waist and secured it tightly under the bed.

He was mumbling in high-pitched, pathetic drones, I couldn't make out what he was going on about. Probably praying or something. He coughed and spluttered occasionally, but I was pretty confident he'd survive the process.

I took a scalpel and sliced him, not too deep, between the straps, down the middle of his chest to the top of his navel. He barely flinched. I knew the coagulant had worked because there was very little blood. I carefully slid my finger into the centre of the cut and hooked it under his skin. The fact that he'd lost so much weight had made the skin nice and loose, and it came away from his insides easier than I'd expected. I ran my finger up and down the incision to form a flap of about an inch or so on either side, then I carefully pulled them open.

I could see his internal organs struggling to fight the coagulant and then stop. He'd gone.

I'd used too much. Due to being deprived of sleep, he simply wasn't well enough to keep fighting. He'd given up. Who could blame him? I realised at this point just how much the buzz of killing had faded. I didn't feel anything at all, the euphoria I'd experienced with Uncle Jack was a distant memory, but I still wanted to finish the job properly, though; I had a message to deliver. So I continued to pull open the skin, being careful to keep the original cut intact; I didn't want to tear the skin at the top and bottom of the incision as it would be harder to put him back together once I'd finished.

I held up the left side and slid in photocopies of the disbelievers' verse from the Koran, carefully wallpapering his insides with it. Once it was tidy and full, I did the same with the other side. Then I Super Glued the wound together as tidily as I could.

I left him down there for a day or so before I moved him. His body was as stiff as a board and I had to lower the back seats and push him through the boot and lay him diagonally across the seats to fit him in the car. I covered him with a blanket and dumped him in the lay-by at Saddleworth where I'd met him over a week before. It didn't take long for him to be found.

ESCAPING
THE AWAKENING

Where am I? What's going on? Why am I here? What is this place? A hospital…? My fucking head… What did I do to end up in here? I can't remember… I remember bits… Just bits…. All bad bits. I can't move my arms… Or my legs. What's going on?

My head and neck feel stiff. I turn my head slowly to the right. It takes all my strength and I hear it creak as it moves. I can see a machine bleeping in the corner. I assume I'm wired up to it. There's nobody else in here and no flowers or anything, so I can't have been here that long. Either that, or nobody's coming to see me.

There must be something in here that'll let me know who I am. I move my head to the left, slowly and carefully. It takes a while, but as it comes to rest on the pillow and I glance at the cabinet to the side of my bed I can see it has three photographs in frames on top of it. The photos look old, tatty and worn; like they weren't always in a frame.

I think that's me on them. I'm on them all, but with someone different on each one. It's hard to focus. I concentrate my efforts on one picture. I'm stood with someone. It's somewhere hot. We both look really happy…

I remember now. I remember being disappointed at my

grades when I finished school. I knew I'd have no chance of passing them after being bounced around from pillar to post, but part of me thought that I deserved a bit of luck. I remember feeling at a loss once school had finished, but excited, too; I'd just turned sixteen, which meant I could break free from the home and fend for myself. I could finally start a real life on my own.

I decided to get a job and took whatever I could. I ended up being a glass collector in a town centre bar. I also decided to go to college. Despite the situation with his mother years earlier, I had remained very good friends with James, who had now decided he liked to be called Jimbob – that's the other face on the picture. It's Jimbob! I knew that if Jimbob was going to college, at least I'd have a friend there. I wanted to do music with him but they wouldn't let me in, so I signed up for a course in Media Studies.

I tried my best but college held just as little interest for me as school had. I wanted to get away. The council was paying for my flat and I'd been saving pretty much every penny I'd earned at the pub. I wasn't used to having any money so I didn't really know what to do with it. I just instinctively saved it. I'd never been abroad before and figured I could use the money to see what it was like. I didn't really fancy going it alone, though. I'd already mentioned it to Jimbob and he'd seemed keen on the idea, but he's one of those people who has a habit of saying whatever he needs to say for a quiet life.

By the time I'd reached the end of the first year, I'd saved what I reckoned would be enough for a decent holiday, but I didn't have the first clue where to go. Then it came to me. I was out with Jimbob one night after college, drinking in a local bar, and I heard a guy at another table bragging to his mates whilst Jimbob was getting the drinks in. Thinking back on it now, he sounded like a right fucking know-it-all bragging prick, but I was entranced. He had one of those public school-like, drawly, posh voices.

"You're going to Ibiza? I just got back last Tuesday, It was fucking awesome, man. Fucking clubs, fucking girls, fucking drugs, you need to go, yeah. Here, take this card, it's for the hotel we stayed in; The Mitjorn. It's just close enough to everything and just far enough away… It's in San Antonio, about a two minute walk from the west end. Although I'd stay away from the fucking west end if I were you, it's full of drunken fucking beer boys that are there to get pissed and pull pleb munters, but you can't hear the racket from the Mitjorn. It's five minutes from the sunset bars, you have to check them out, and just down the way there's a bar called the Pussycat that does a good deal on all the club tickets. I think it's supposed to be a gay bar but I didn't give a fuck! You definitely need to do Space on Sunday and Pacha on the Monday, Sanchez is on. It's fucking awesome, man, you'll want to dress up for that one; it's a bit posher than the rest.

"Then have a couple of days off, that'd be a good time to go down to the sunset bars. Don't bother with Café Del Mar, though – too commercial since the song, and at least two euros more for a drink than anywhere else. Go to Mambo, Kanya or Savannah, in fact go to Kanya during the day, you've never seen as many fit birds in one place at one time. Then on Thursday go to Amnesia, its Cream's night, Van Dyke will be on and probably Helliwell too. Fucking banging. Fridays are shite, maybe go to the west end for a cheap night out if you're bored. Its wank but it's your only real chance of getting a shag. Saturday… El Da Vino, Head Kandi. Really nice club, clientele's a bit too cool for school but it's worth going for the club and the tunes. Then have Sunday off, get something to eat.

David's is pretty good, too, but if you fancy splashing out, try Villa Mercedes, it's just across from the hotel. The food's not amazing but it's good and the atmosphere's wicked. Monday, go to Manumission. It's like a fucking circus, the music will probably be shite but the club is fucking awesome, man, you need to see it. You can go on other nights but they close half of the fucker off so you can't see it properly. Then chill out till your flight home. It won't be a comedown – it'll be a fucking crash down. You'll feel like shite – be dizzy, have head shocks, feel paranoid, but it won't matter... Because you'll be chilling by the fucking pool knowing you've got four or five days of doing fuck all before you have to go home.

You're going to need some serious coin, too. You're looking at around fifty euros to get into a club then, depending where it is, between ten and forty in a taxi to get there. Drinks in the clubs will set you back at least ten, closer to twenty if you're on spirits. And the drugs... Best thing to do is just see the lucky-lucky men. They're all over the place, the black guys, they'll probably ask you if you want anything, so you shouldn't need to go looking. Never accept their first price. You'll usually be able to get pills for three or four euros and more often than not they're pretty good – not amazing, but good enough, yeah? Weed will cost you twenty, it's usually resin and it's shite but beggars can't be choosers. The coke isn't worth bothering with, the quality is okay if you're lucky, but at best it's only okay. You only get about a third of gram, though, and even if you haggle like fuck with them, you'll be lucky to get it for less than forty – but... You'll buy it anyway, just like every fucker else does. You'll have a fucking mint time, man, I'm telling you. I just wish I could afford to go back with you. Come see me when you get back and tell me all about it, yeah?"

I scribbled all the details down on a beer mat as quickly as I could and when Jimbob got back from the bar, I sounded him out about going. He resisted at first but there was no way I was backing down. I knew Jimbob better than anyone and provided I kept chipping away at him, sooner or later he'd end up caving in. So, of course, a week later we were on a plane.

I remember the feeling of excitement that bubbled inside me as I looked out of the small aeroplane window into the pitch black night, marvelling at the fact that I was in the air. This was my first time flying abroad and I wanted to soak up every inch of it. Even the crap meal, over-priced drinks and uncontrollable wind couldn't wipe the grin off my face. I just sat there looking pleasantly bemused for the full two and a half hours.

When we touched down and I got off the plane, it didn't have one of those long corridor things that they had in England that lead between the plane and the airport, so we had to walk down some stairs and head for a bus to the arrivals area. The air I was breathing in was hot and sticky, thick and strange. I'd never felt or tasted anything like it in my lungs or mouth before. I felt frustrated as I waited by the carousel for my bags to arrive, and when they did finally turn up, I was frustrated again at having to queue for a taxi for what seemed like an eternity. I barely spoke to Jimbob the whole way to the Mitjorn, I just looked out of the windows at my surroundings. A strange mix of barren wasteland littered with billboards advertising club nights, that occasionally gave way to small hubs of activity and bars with neon lights and drinks promotions, then a long road, five or ten minutes of little or nothing, until I saw a huge, crystal-shaped dome on the horizon to the right. I asked the cab driver what it was and he told me it was Privilege, the club where Manumission was held. I felt giddy with excitement and then, before I knew it, I heard music, loud banging music and I turned my head to the left to see Amnesia.

This was all so new, so perfect. I knew I could be anybody I wanted here. Nobody would know me. Nobody would know my past. To everyone I met, I'd be normal, for the first time in my life. I was almost dizzy with the anticipation.

The activity outside the cab died down for another few minutes before I got a closer look at Privilege, to the right on the way past, then another five or ten minutes and in the horizon I could see what looked like a large egg. As we approached, it I realised it was the centrepiece of a roundabout and, as we passed it, San Antonio unfolded in front of me. I know it too well to notice now, but on first glance, it just looked like beautiful women everywhere, bars, clubs, shops, restaurants and a smile on everyone's face. I know now it isn't as pretty as the memory, but that was what I felt and thought at first.

We ran along the left-hand side of these shops and restaurants and at the other side I could see a harbour. The road turned to the right, and in front of me I saw a mass of drunken, rowdy people and assumed (correctly) that I was looking up into the west end. I thought for a moment that the cab driver was going to take us straight through it, but instead, he took a left away from the hustle and bustle and within twenty seconds everywhere around us was almost silent. We passed a couple of closed clothes shops, until a left turn took us to the back entrance of our hotel.

We split the cab fair, the driver helped us out with our cases and slowly we approached the Mitjorn. A guy called Tony was there to meet us. At the time, I thought Tony must have been stoned or something, although I found out later that he was teetotal. He got us a drink and when we asked to check in, he blurted out in his crazy Spanish accent, "Drink first. I can't be arsed doing the paperwork." We liked him instantly and did as we were told and had a couple of beers and played a game of pool.

Once he'd finally got around to checking us in an hour or so later, we went up to our room. Part of me wanted to go straight out and party, but it all seemed a little too intimidating so I decided it'd be better to get some sleep, wait and see what tomorrow had in store for us.

Jimbob drifted off straightaway. I couldn't sleep, though. I remember being told about a child's excitement on Christmas Eve night and wondered if this was me finally getting to experience what it felt like. Nothing had excited me more in my life than the endless possibilities that would be waiting for me once I woke up. I pictured myself dancing in clubs and talking to good-looking girls. I wondered if I'd be forced to do drugs and worried if anything might happen to me if I tried. I hoped the four hundred euros spending money I'd brought would be enough to last the ten days and I thought, above all else, that this could be a fresh start to a new me.

As the morning came and sleep left me, the excitement returned and I was eager to face the day ahead. It was Saturday. Once we'd got up and had a bit of toast, courtesy of Tony's sister who ran the bar during the day, I went outside and sat in heat I'd never experienced by the side of the pool and reeled off the list of club nights I'd jotted down to Jimbob. Jimbob didn't really seem to care, and his lack of excitement really pissed me off at the time. Not that I let him know; we were going to be out there a fair old while and I didn't see the point in causing any friction. We made no decisions on what we were going to do, we just simply sat in the warm sun and steadily enjoyed a few beers.

A few hours, a few beers and half a bottle of sun cream later, we were approached by a guy who had his bags packed and was ready to leave. He had a Welsh accent and looked high as a fucking kite. "Alright there, boys. First day, is it?"

Jimbob nodded as I squinted up at him.

"Last day for me, you see. I'm fucking flying back home tonight. Thing is, I can't take all this shit with me, so do you want it?"

He placed a small, suspicious-looking cash bag on the table and said, "It's not much, like, but it'll save you a few quid. Better than the crap you can get out here. I brought my own with me, like. But it's too risky taking it back. About half a gram of Charlie and six pills in there. I fancied doing the Charlie in before I left, but I've not slepped properly for a fucking week and want to get my head down on the plane, you see. Have it all, you're welcome to it."

For a second, Jimbob looked as if he was going to decline, and although I'd never taken anything before, I was definitely curious. I butted straight in and quickly accepted before Jimbob had a chance to reject the offer. I thanked the guy, showed him the list of club nights we'd been looking at, told him how much cash we had and asked which nights to go for. He told us to do Space on the Sunday and Amnesia on the Thursday. Told us to do El Da Vino the following Saturday if we had the cash left, rather than doing it straight away and feeling like shit for Space. It all seemed to make sense in a nonsensical kind of way.

When the guy left, Jimbob confronted me about the drugs. "What the fuck did you take them for? We're not fucking druggies!"

I didn't want to get into an argument with him, but I was fucked if I was coming all this way and not experiencing the whole thing properly, so I decided to tentatively nudge him along to my way of thinking. "I know, but aren't you curious, just a little?"

"Well, yeah," he admitted, "but I've never done anything before. What if it kills us?"

"Well, I was thinking about that when I took them off him. If he's been taking this stuff all week and he's okay, at least we know that they're safe, I suppose. Better than just buying them from anyone. We'd have no idea what we were getting then, would we?"

"I suppose…"

"Shall we try one of those pills?"

"Fuck off!"

"Come on, let's split one. We can have one now and see what it's like."

"We're supposed to be going to that Space place tomorrow. Why don't we wait and have one then? Everyone else will be on them there, too, I reckon. I don't want to do one now by the side of a pool during the day, it'll be a waste of time."

I was a bit pissed off that Jimbob was being such a killjoy, but I knew he was right. It would be better to wait. So we went back upstairs and stashed the small bag in our room, then headed off out of the hotel to get familiar with our surroundings.

We bought the tickets for Space and Amnesia straight away from a shop literally just outside the back entrance to the hotel. This way, we knew that we'd definitely not spend too much to be unable to go; even if we did blow our cash, we were covered for the club nights. We followed the signs towards the beach and were quite surprised when we got to it as it was just a load more bars spilling out onto some rough-looking rocks. We followed them along past Café Del Mar and a place called Mambo's until we reached the bar called Kanya that the bloke had mentioned in the pub the week before. I remembered what he'd said and suggested that we chill out there for a while.

So we had a few more drinks. Jimbob was moaning about how much money we'd spent already and how much more the holiday would cost and, although he had a point, I just wanted to enjoy the moment and not worry about what we were spending; it was worth every penny.

I remember looking around at the packed pool area and beach front and saying to Jimbob, "How much would you pay if a bird came up to you and asked how much you'd be willing to fork out to see her tits in the flesh?"

Jimbob laughed. "What?"

"How much? Some fit bird walks up to you right now and says, 'Here, you can see my tits'. -What would you pay?"

"I dunno... A fiver?"

"Well... Look, just look out there, there must be at least a hundred fucking fit birds out there, all of them with their tits out. So you've got your money's worth already, haven't you? And it gets better, because we'll see fucking hundreds more before we leave, too. All shapes and sizes. Look at the variety on offer out there. Small ones, big ones, pert ones, false ones, saggy ones, small nips, big nips, soft nips, hard nips – it's like a pick and mix of tits right there in front of you for your viewing pleasure, and for fucking free! Shit, man! We need to get some fucking mirrored shades!"

We both shared a laugh and he seemed to chill out a bit. We ordered the best chocolate milkshake I've ever tasted in my life and relaxed, enjoying the rest of the day. Then, as the day drew to a close, we headed back to the hotel to eat, drink some more, and rest in preparation for Space.

When we woke up and started getting ready, we realised that we had absolutely no idea of what sort of clothes we should be wearing. It seemed odd that a club would open at ten in the morning. We opted to dress in gear that was half way between daytime and night time attire. Three quarter pants with a shirt. We dressed similarly; at least then, if we were wrong in what we'd chosen, we'd be wrong together and both look like twats.

Then followed the panic of what to do with the drugs. What to take. Where to hide it. We decided to go for thc safe option and take a single pill each; swallow it just before we went in. At least that way, even if we did get searched, the bouncers wouldn't find anything and refuse us entry – we couldn't afford to waste money by not getting into nights we'd already paid for. Not to mention the seventy or eighty euros the return taxi would set us back.

Once we arrived at the club, we stood and looked at it from the outside. I don't know what I expected but what I saw wasn't it. I think I expected something huge, grand and awe-inspiring, but it seemed modest from the outside and there wasn't even a queue.

We'd clearly got there pretty early, but once we got inside, something awe-inspiring opened out in front of us. The only club we'd ever seen up until this time was the little shite hole in the middle of Holme Bridge, but this was unfathomably huge to us. As we walked towards the bar a hundred yards or so in front of us, I could see people sat to the left, chilling out on massage chairs, and a crowd of people to the right dancing to some DJ in a booth high above the back of the dance floor. I ordered a Jack Daniels and Coke and was too preoccupied to worry about the ridiculous amount it had just cost me.

We wondered onto the dance floor and stood amongst the revellers in a crowd which seemed to be multiplying by the second. Fowning our drinks as quickly as we could, we navigated our way through the ever-growing mass of sweaty bodies to place the empties on the bar, before squeezing back through and taking our spot back at the heart of the dance floor. We started to move – feeling the now familiar, but then so new and fresh, tingling of the Ecstasy knocking on the door of our consciousness, asking politely to be let in.

Four or five songs later and there were bodies as far as the eye could see, all united in one purpose, to move, to dance, to enjoy – and then, as the tune broke and the breakdown kicked in, I raised my hands and the Ecstasy washed over my entire body in a single euphoric wave. I shivered and gasped for breath and then the music smashed back in. I could feel it hit me, like I was descending on a thrill ride. I turned round to look at Jimbob and grabbed him. I hugged him and we jumped together to the music.

*

I don't remember much after that. I'm assuming we carried on partying until the cash we brought out that day pretty much ran out; which can't have taken long. But it didn't matter, we partied so hard on the days following that by the time we got into our second week, we physically couldn't manage to party any more even if we'd wanted to. The drugs we were so impressed with for not giving us 'hangovers' earlier in the week had taken their toll, and we were soon snappy and irritable.

We slept for pretty much two days solid, only surfacing to take it in turns to trek downstairs to the bar and get more water or packets of crisps. Jesus! From Space up until that point, I don't think we'd even eaten; well, hardly eaten, anyway. We'd ordered a sandwich or a pizza over the few days of our drug-fuelled stupor, but not managed more than a couple of mouthfuls. We were running on empty.

And so were our wallets. Thankfully, my wage went in on a Thursday, which meant that we only had to get through a couple of days of lounging around by the pool skint, before I could get to a cash point and draw us out enough for one final blow-out. We decided to have that blow-out in San Antonio and, rather than going to a club, we'd go to the sunset bars. Our holiday was nearly over and we'd still not seen one of those sunsets that everyone went on so much about.

We lounged around throughout the day and went to get ready to go out pretty early that day. Early start, early finish kind of thing. It was our last full night and we flew back the day after, so we wanted to get some proper sleep before being turfed out of our room at ten in the morning.

Once we were ready, we tidied everything away and packed our stuff up; another precaution to secure us those all important extra few minutes of sleep the following morning. Then we set off on a stroll to the beach.

Once there, we plonked ourselves down on the rocks and had a few drinks whilst we sat and waited for the evening to draw in. As the day dissolved away and the sun began to descend over the small rocks in the sea on the horizon, the beach began to crowd up. Ambient music was discretely pumping out, complemented by the sound of the waves softly licking the rock shore. To our left, a woman juggled with fire in front of a few entranced spectators and to our right, people danced and giggled. As the base of the sun hit the top of the rocks, the DJ mixed in another tune, this time more sombre, more moving. I looked out at the sea in front of me, glowing golden from the reflection of the setting sun flickering across its small rippling waves, and thought about the week we'd had. Not a care in the world, a non-stop party. We'd had to answer to nobody. It was the first time in my life that I'd not been worried or stressed. I remembered Space and us grabbing each other when that first pill took hold, and then I did something I'd promised all those years ago in the home that I'd never do – I started blubbing. Not uncontrollably or anything, just small tears welling up in my eyes which, thankfully, were hidden by my sunglasses.

I turned to Jimbob and told him I didn't want to leave, and I could see from his face that his glasses were covering up the same emotion as I was feeling. He said he didn't want to go home, either, and then it struck me. We didn't need to fucking go. We weren't due back in college for another five weeks. We could stay. We could definitely stay. We'd met enough mad heads out there to get a job selling tickets, or dragging people into bars. We sat and we talked about it, and as we shook hands and agreed that we were staying, the sun disappeared behind the rocks and the ambient music disappeared in a flash and was replaced by the banging house that had pretty much become our diet for the last couple of weeks.

We leapt to our feet and jumped to the music. It felt like the first day all over again we were giddy with excitement and anticipation, just as we had been ten days before. We needed to get jobs, we needed money, we needed to find somewhere to stay. All things that, by rights, should have freaked us out, but not that night. That night we forgot all that.

*

Within a couple of days, we were sorted. We found a job selling tickets for a sunset cruise, and the owner, a bloke named Charro, gave us an apartment as part of our pay. It was a shite hole, mind you. And we were only raking in a commission of a euro between us for every ticket we sold, which was crap, really, considering he charged fifty euros a piece for them. It did net us a good fifty euros each a day, though, which was a hell of a lot more than a lot of other people got for their jobs – particularly when you considered we were living rent free.

Still, it wasn't enough for us to carry on going out clubbing every night like we'd wanted. It didn't matter so much, though, as we found ways of making extra cash by finding pills for the party goers and skimming cash of the top, but by the time we'd eaten and stuff, we were still left pretty skint. Ibiza was fucking expensive, man.

We worked with a guy called Gez from Bristol, who got vocal with Charro about how much we were being ripped off on our commission, and he just disappeared one day. I assumed that he'd taken off to another part of the island in a huff with Charro, but we saw him a week or so later hobbling about the resort on fucking crutches. He'd told us he was lucky to get off with a beating; plenty of people before him had just disappeared altogether apparently.

Gez couldn't afford to get home and didn't have anywhere to stay. On top of this, he had no travel insurance and couldn't pay the bill for having his legs broken. I was furious, so I put a little plan in place for us to exact some revenge on fucking Charro. Jimbob took some convincing and whined like a little bitch about it for a while, but I managed to convince him that what we needed to do was for the best for us.

So, this particular day, Jimbob and I went out selling the tickets and we fucking sold our arses off. The sunset cruise had a capacity of two hundred but we shifted over a thousand. That was over fifty thousand euros. We headed over to Charro's apartment and bust through the door, before turfing his belongings everywhere and making the place look like a shit hole.

Then we decided to do a little redecorating. We took some paint we'd found in the bottom of one of his cupboards and drew a picture of an aeroplane on the wall, with the words *HA, HA, HA* underneath it, and took pictures of ourselves posing in front of it holding massive wads of the money with a camera we'd found lying around, before discarding it on the floor with the rest of the rubbish, leaving, getting our belongings, heading off out to meet Gez and getting the fuck off the island.

We didn't leave by plane as we'd suggested in the picture, though. Oh no. Too much waiting around, and the airport would be the first place he'd go to look. We were too smart for that and headed to the harbour. Within an hour, we'd already set sail for Barcelona and we had a fucking shit-load of money.

We giggled as we thought of the look on his face as a thousand angry punters turned up for a trip that that they'd paid for, and pissed ourselves at the thought of how angry he'd be when he got to his apartment and saw the mess we'd made of it. Then we almost pissed our pants, laughing so hard at the thought of him developing the pictures in the camera, perhaps a few months down the line when he'd just forgotten all about it.

This had been fun, and Charro had deserved it but it was almost too simple. Jimbob really buzzed off it, actually. I feared he might have got a taste for robbery. We kept it sensible, though; we knew we had to take precautions to make sure he couldn't track us down easily, so we agreed to split the cash, split up and travel Europe for a couple of weeks, then all head back home at different times. I wouldn't head back to Holme Bridge with Jimbob as originally intended, I'd go back to Bracknell instead. It would be hard to track him down as he used a nickname, but easy to track us if we were both together in the same place. I'd just have to lie low for a while and come back when we knew the coast was clear.

JUSTICE
THE AWAKENING

She's sat up on the bed, the covers are over her legs but her breasts are exposed. This is irritating me beyond belief, as someone I've never seen or met before but understand to be her ex-boyfriend is sitting on the bed next to me.

It seems that we're in a relationship and going through some kind of rough patch, but I have absolutely no idea as to why. I want to tell her to cover herself up but I've lost too many good relationships through jealousy and a strong tendency to be possessive, so I've taught myself to resist any urges to say anything under circumstances such as these. I can feel the jealousy sliding into my heart and the pit of my stomach like a serrated knife, and twisting. I feel my throat tightening and hurting as I use all my power to keep the thoughts inside my mind from clumsily spilling out of my lips.

I try to rationalise. If I can rationalise this it'll dilute the pain. He's her ex-boyfriend. It's not like he hasn't seen her breasts before; probably a hundred times. Why would this time be anything different? She's just innocently sat up and thought nothing of it, most likely. Or has she? Does she want him to see them? Is she testing me to see whether or not I act jealous, or is she trying to turn him on? If I was in his situation, I'd be turned on. You're losing it – rationalise. Women aren't like men though, they don't realise how sexually charged we are. They seem to have a blissful naivety about it all, they'll happily show you some scar on the top of their thigh and think that a man's interest will be genuine, but he's secretly perving over her flesh. Yes, I must admit that, in the split second it takes to aim a slight smile at an attractive girl as she passes by, I've undressed them, fucked them, re-dressed them, cracked them on the arse, and sent them on their way. What if it's just me that thinks like that, though? What if other people don't think like me? Maybe that's why some people don't suffer with jealousy – because they don't think like I do. I'm losing it again. I need to get out of here without it looking as if I'm in a huff. I ask them if either of them would like a cup of tea or coffee and they both want a tea. I leave calmly, collectedly, and once I close the door behind me I collapse, exhausted from keeping my feelings in.

I don't know why we're going through such a rough patch. Why can't all this just be simple? At least a little continuity when I see her from time to time, instead of jumping in and out of random situations. This one's new, though. Up until now, I've met her and had to try and find somewhere to have sex with her, but this time we're in an established relationship and something's wrong. I pick myself up off the floor and head to the kitchen to make the drinks.

I can see a neon flicker coming from an oven placed at a slightly higher level on the wall to my head. It occurs to me that it's a ridiculously unpractical place to keep an oven, considering the damage the heat could do to a person's eyes, but I've learned to ignore minor randomnesses such as this. As I open it, I can see it's a small, glowing frog. Very small, no bigger than my thumbnail, it's that whitey green colour that glow-in-the-dark kids' toys are. I hold out my hand and it jumps into my palm. I head through a door into the garden and place the frog carefully on the grass. At the back of the garden, I can see a large rabbit struggling to climb a step that separates the garden from a park, and I decide to give it a hand but, as I approach it, I feel scared to help it in case it attacks me. I take a deep breath and grab it by the scruff of the neck. It's heavy and huge, at least the size of a full bin liner, but I manage to lift it and place it in the park.

I turn back around to see that she's now dressed and sitting in the garden alone. She doesn't look mad at me any more and she says she wants to show me something. She takes me by the hand and leads me back into where the kitchen was, but it's now a living room with wicker furniture and a small hi-fi.

She sits me in a wicker rocking chair and turns on the music system. She presses play and music begins – a strong and powerful orchestral number, almost like the score for an epic film. This is the first time I've actually heard anything in a dream. Ever. Usually, I know what's going on instinctively, like a kind of telepathy, but I never actually hear anything. I can now, though – I can hear it as plain as day. It's powerful, emotional, not the sort of thing I'd usually like, but for some reason I'm in awe. She tells me it's her composition and she's written it for me and then she smiles and walks towards me. I'm hypnotized by her beauty and, as she approaches me, I get up from the chair, reach out my arms and she holds me; she holds me so tightly, and even though this is one of our least sexual encounters so far, it's definitely the best yet.

Up until now, our relationship has been based on lust but this time it's love. An overwhelming, powerful and intense feeling of contentment and commitment. I've loved her for a long time but the difference today is that she loves me, too. As she holds me, everything around us fizzles away. We're stood – it looks like we're floating because nothing surrounds us any more but the sensation is still one of standing – embraced, with this epic

126

score in the background. I want this to last forever.

Why? Why the fuck can't I just stay there? Pull yourself together, man! You're crying over someone that doesn't even exist. But I love her. I really love her. Doesn't matter, come on. Get your shit together. Yes, I just need to sort my own head out. I've got a busy day. Calm down… Deep breaths… Right… Fine… Shit, shower and a shave and get to the station.

*

Oh, for fuck's sake. The boss has dragged me into his office, probably going to bollock me for going to see Tim, I reckon, or to have another go about me hanging around with Julie. It looks surprisingly tidy in here, for a change, I can actually see his desk; it's usually littered with paper.

Here we go, I can see him coming.

"Right, I need you to do me a favour, Scott," he says. I'm immediately relieved that this doesn't look like it'll be a telling-off – but, to be honest, I don't have either the time or the inclination to be doing anyone any favours at the moment.

He continues. "I wouldn't ask if there was anyone else available, but we're spread pretty thin around here at the moment and it needs doing, I'm afraid."

"What? What needs doing?"

"You remember when the bank in town got robbed a few years back?"

"Yeah."

"Well, the only guy who survived the robbery's been in a coma for the last four years and he's woken up. I just need you to interview him."

Oh, I can't be fucking arsed with this. "Can't someone from uniform do it?"

"Well, yes, they can, but I'd like you to do it. You're a better

127

interviewer than most of those, plus you have to remember that you're still technically in training. I would have been telling you to do it rather than asking, if we were running normally down here."

"By the sound of it, you *are* telling me and not asking me."

"Well… Yeah I suppose I am, but I'm trying to go about it in a decent way. Please don't make me have to act like a cunt about this."

You are a cunt. "Fine. When do you want me to go?"

"As soon as. You might as well get it out of the way."

"Yeah, I don't know anything about the case, though. Is this going to take loads of reading up on first, because I'm really pushed for time."

"Nah, he's claiming amnesia, apparently. I just want you to let me know whether or not you think he's telling porkies. You're good at seeing through people, that's another reason it's best that you do the interview. Don't be too heavy on him or anything, keep it relatively informal. You don't need to be in there for hours, just ten or fifteen minutes."

Like I've nothing fucking better to do... "Fine, I'll do it this afternoon."

"Can you do it this morning?"

Talk about a fucking piss-take. "Yeah, I'll do it straight way then."

"Here's the file. You don't need to read it, just skim it."

Don't worry, I've got no intention of reading it. "Okay."

I pick Julie up on my way over to the hospital, and whilst I drive, I tell her briefly about my meeting with Tim. I also tell her that everything is off the record until the investigation's over, but she tries to put my mind at rest by telling me that she wasn't intending putting anything she found out as a result of us working together into the *Gazette*. Instead, she was writing a fucking book about it. I should be bothered, but I couldn't care less, to be honest; that book will definitely put both me and the force in a positive light.

I ask her to flick through the file for this guy we're going to see, check if there's anything in there she'd like to know, but she seems as uninterested in this chore as I do.

As we pull up outside Holme Bridge General, I remember my first meeting with Julie those few weeks ago and chuckle to myself.

"What's so funny?" she asks as we exit the car.

"Well, do you remember when I came to interview you in here?"

"Not brilliantly, in all honesty. I was a bit out of it."

I laugh again. "Yeah, I know"

"What's that supposed to mean?"

"Do you remember what you said to me? Your first words?"

"Not really, no."

I laugh louder. "You said, 'There's only two types of copper. A new copper or a bent copper. Which are you?'"

She manages to crack a smile and says, "Well, can you blame me? I thought it was a fucking copper that had taken me."

"So what do you think now?" I ask

"What do you mean?"

"Am I a new copper? Or am I a bent copper?"

She laughs; she has a nice, genuine-sounding laugh. Not at all forced. She keeps her mouth closed so it's almost like a series of hums. She looks down, away from me, too. It's quite cute. "Why don't you tell me what kind of copper you are."

"Well… I'm a copper that believes in what he's doing. I'm not really in either of your categories. I'm a copper that just, you know, wants to solve crime."

"Bollocks!"

"I'm serious. Why else would I be doing what I'm doing? I've worked really hard to get where I am at my age. It was all well and good in uniform, but I was reacting and preventing crime and that wasn't for me. I want to *solve* crime. It's an interest for me. I genuinely like my job. Except this bit. I don't much like being dragged off to work on a case that was pretty much shut years ago."

"And what is your age?"

"I'm twenty-six."

"You look older." She does that laugh again.

"Oh… Thanks."

"Anyway, the case isn't closed. It said so in the file."

"Huh?"

"Well apparently, when this guy did the robbery, he told the cashier said he seemed coerced. He might know something."

"What's his name again?"

"Did you even read this report?"

"Erm… I skimmed it."

"Bullshit. You didn't even look, did you?"

Oh fuck. I hope that doesn't end up in her book. "I skimmed it."

"Well, if you'd skimmed a bit closer, you'd see that he wasn't found with any identification and his description didn't fit any police profiles. He's what the Americans would call a John Doe."

"Right."

We're here, stood just outside the door to his room. It must have cost a fair bit, keeping someone in a private room at an NHS hospital all these years. I wonder who's been picking up the bill? Julie grabs the handle and is just about to walk in before me when I loosely grab her harm. "I'd best go in alone first and ask if it's okay for you to be in there. Do you mind?"

"No, of course not. I'll wait here."

As I go in, I can already see that this guy can't really be up to speaking to anyone; he looks in a bad way and, as I approach his bed, I'm uncertain of how to start the conversation. An introduction makes sense.

"Hello. I'm Scott Dempsey. I'm with Holme Bridge CID. Are you up to answering a few questions?"

His eyes roll towards me but he's otherwise motionless. "I suppose so. Why?" His voice is croaky; it's to be expected, I guess. My voice sounds croaky when I wake up on a morning after a night's kip; this guys been asleep for years!

"Do you mind if I bring in someone who's working with me? She's not a police officer, she's a reporter, but she'll be happy to keep everything confidential."

"Erm… Yeah, whatever."

I head off to the door and motion Julie in. She sits down in a chair at the back of the room and says nothing.

"What's this all about?" he croaks.

"Well," I say, "I was hoping to be able to ask you the same question. Can you remember why you're in here?"

"No. I can't remember much at all, to be honest."

"Okay, let's start with something easier then. Can you remember your name?"

"Yeah, yeah I can remember that. My name's Jonathan."

"Surname?"

"Thorpe."

I jot the name down. It rings no bells. "So, Mr Thorpe, what about your date of birth?"

"Fifteenth of August, nineteen-eighty-one."

"And where do you live?"

He looks up, purses his lips slightly, then after a few seconds he relaxes to meet my gaze and says, "I don't know."

"What's the last thing you do remember?"

"Being about seventeen-years-old. Living in Ibiza."

"Ibiza? You're a far cry from Ibiza now, mate. Anything else? Anything more recent?"

"No. Why? Am I in trouble? Did I do something wrong?"

"Honestly, I don't know."

"Well, what do you know?"

"I can't really tell you what I know, Mr Thorpe. We need your memory to come back of its own accord, rather than you forcing it, or me influencing it in any way."

Then Julie lifts her head from the file and says, "Does the name Tarquin mean anything to you?"

"No," he replies.

I butt in to prevent Julie from asking any more questions. "Look, is there anything else at all you can remember. Anything more recent? Think."

He looks agitated now. "I've done nothing but think," he says, "and I can't remember anything past being seventeen. I wish I could! I can't even remember how to move my arms or legs! Or take a fucking shit! I can't eat properly. Believe me, I want to know who I am more than anyone."

"Well, is there anyone I can contact that you remember from back then? Someone that might jog your memory? Now we have your name, we could contact your parents, perhaps."

"No point," he says. "My mum's dead and my dad's in jail. And I don't want him knowing where I am. He won't care, anyway."

"Anyone else?"

"No."

"Okay, well, I'll leave you to it in that case, Mr Thorpe. See if I can do a bit of digging and perhaps find someone who might be able to help you. I'll see you in a couple of days."

"All right. See you."

I leave the room, closely followed by Julie. "Do you think he was telling the truth?" she asks.

"Yeah. I reckon, anyway. If he wasn't, he's a fucking genius at body language for someone who can only control his head. He seemed genuine enough to me."

"So what are you going to do?"

"I don't know. Suppose I'll run a check on his name tomorrow. Why did you ask that question about the name… Tarquin, was it?"

"Yeah. Three days after that crash, a guy called Tarquin never showed up for work again. Some of the work force think he ran off with some lottery syndicate money, or was supposed to put it on some tickets and didn't, or whatever. This Tarquin guy's boss came in to try and identify our Dave Thorpe and said he'd never heard of him, but it seemed a bit coincidental that this guy disappears at the same time as our guy ends up in a car wreck."

"I suppose. We'll have a look into it, but first we've got more important business to attend to."

"Like what?"

"Breakfast. I'm fucking starving. You going to let me treat you to a full cooked English?"

*

We ate at a local café and scrutinized the coma guy's files some more before heading to the station to do a little digging on the name he gave us: 'Jonathan Thorpe'. Unfortunately, the searches on the system threw up a lot more questions than answers, and although I really couldn't be arsed dealing with any of it, Julie was pretty persistent in solving the riddle surrounding him.

We looked over the case files again regarding my serial killer theory, and Julie's convinced I'm on the right track, but we don't have a shred of hard evidence to link the murders. We found some DNA on Julie, but it came up with no matches and without a sample from the killer, there's absolutely no way we can pair the two up. I'm still not one hundred percent convinced that Julie was a potential victim, but her hazy description of being kept in a room with some odd-looking pets could potentially explain some of the seemingly unexplainable ways in which some of the victims have been drugged, or poisoned, or whatever.

I wanted to tell her that I think Tim Morris is the next likely suspect, and I also wanted to let her know that I wanted him to die for what he'd done, but I kept shtum. I have to remember sometimes that, as friendly as we might be, she is still a reporter. The thing is, I get the impression that she's keeping something from me, too. She's very conscious of every conversation and seems to handle both her responses and questions in an extremely controlled manner. Hopefully, I'll be able to break down these barriers tonight. I've arranged to meet her for a few drinks in the village. It was her suggestion, actually, she reckoned I needed to let my hair down and relax, told me I was probably too close to the problem to solve it. She used a bit of an odd analogy, something like, "You're too caught up in all this to be able to look at it objectively. Like when you're doing a crossword puzzle and you sit for ages scratching your head over a question you know the answer to. Then an hour later, when you're sat having a shit, it comes to you. You need to get your mind into a detached and relaxed state and stop concentrating so hard, then you'll figure out what to do. I'll help you. Let's go out and get pissed tonight."

She was right about me not relaxing enough, for sure. I can't remember the last time I went out. My life revolves around work, trying for ages to get to sleep, waking up and wishing I still fucking was asleep, and then going to work again. Jesus, I'm a fucking loser. It's no wonder I'm obsessed over some bird that doesn't even exist; I've got sod all else going on my life.

I feel nervous. It's been ages since I went out. I'm not nervous about meeting Julie, I'm nervous at the thought of possibly meeting some prick that I might have arrested. I can't be arsed with any trouble and it'll go down like a cup of cold sick if I twat someone that has a go.

*

Urgh. Jesus, I'm fucking arseholed. Julie Newton can fair old fucking knock them back, like. I've been matching her drink for drink and here I am with my head over a fucking toilet, spewing, whilst she's out there looking perfectly normal.

I hate this loose feeling in my jaw. I can feel the saliva clagging in preparation for another eruption. Don't fight it, it'll only hurt, or end up coming out of your fucking nose or something. Just let it come...

Ugh. Oh that's better. You need to sort your head out, mate. Get some fucking coke, that'll straighten you out no problem.

No. Nope, can't do it. I'm a copper now.

Fuck off! Couple of cheeky lines and you'll be fine.

No, I'm supposed to be representing the force properly, especially in Julie's company.

Fuck that, you need to get some, not enough to get you wired or anything, just enough to straighten your bonce out. Come on...

No, no, no, no, no, no, no, no, *no*! That's why I've not had a fucking drink for so long. Every time I get pissed, I have to wrestle with myself over cocaine! Right. I'd best wash my face, I bet I stink of fucking rancid bile now, but hey! On the plus side, at least now I've thrown up, I should be able to communicate with my own mouth and motor functions better.

I wait for a while and listen, just to make sure there's nobody lurking outside the cubicle door who'll see me freshening up. All clear, good, a quick swish around my mouth with some water from the sink, then I wash my hands and head back to the bar.

She's sitting over there where I left her, and I focus my eyes before returning and slumping into my seat by her side.

"You took your time," she says, smirking at me.

"Yeah, sorry." I can hear my voice slurring but I can't do anything about it.

She stares at me for a second or so and grins. "You look a bit peaky. Have you been sick?"

"Erm, well I'm not really used to drinking, you see."

"Ha! You're a fucking lightweight. We've only been out for a couple of hours."

"Laugh it up, Julie, but some of us don't have time to be going out and getting pissed."

"Bollocks. You can't even keep up with me. I'm a girl, you're supposed to be able to drink me under the table."

I take a swig of my Jack and Coke. "Yeah, well, obviously not, eh? But that was just round one. Now I've got that vom out of the way, I've got my second wind, so let's get some chasers!" I say, but as I attempt to get to my feet I trip over a bar stool and end up on my arse. I try to lift myself up with the table and manage to tilt it over, covering myself in Julie's G and T and my own Jack and Coke. She escapes the topple unscathed and looks down at me, pissing herself laughing.

"I think we'd better get you home," she says and stands up, reaching her arm out.

I grab it and she helps me pull myself to my feet before supporting me with her arm. I tell her I'll be okay but she insists on taking me home. I feel like a proper fucking cock.

*

I'm slumped on my sofa and she's in the kitchen. Did I pay for the cab? I can't remember. I hear her shout, "Where do you keep your glasses?"

"Erm, cupboard under the sink. Hey! Let me give you some money for that cab!"

She laughs. "You paid the cab yourself!"

She returns and passes me a glass of water, "Here you go. Drink that."

"Thanks."

Coke… No… Coke… No…

"You're funny. I can't believe you got so pissed so quickly."

"Yeah, sorry. Listen, let me give you some money for the cab."

Coke… No… Coke… No…

She leans over and looks at me, carefully swipes my fringe away from my eyes, meets my gaze and says, "For the tenth time – you paid for the cab. Now listen, are you going to be okay if I go home now, or do you want me to hang around for a bit?"

"It's up to you. What do you want to do?"

"I'm easy. Saturday tomorrow, so no work. I'll hang about for a bit if you want. Whatever."

"Cool, thanks."

"My pleasure," she says before leaning in to hold me. Am I reading the signals wrong here? Is this a come-on?

Of course it's a come-on. You need to respond, make a move.

No, I can't, it'd be wrong.

Bullshit! Kiss her, you've got the perfect excuse if she pulls away; you just apologise for being arseholed and call her a cab.

I lift my head from her shoulder slowly and as I move away,

our cheeks meet. I'm deliberately slow, to give her plenty of time to pull away before I get to her lips, but she doesn't flinch. I slowly move to the side and I kiss her, softly, with my mouth closed, carefully checking her response. Is this reciprocal? Was the kiss enough to make her realise that it wasn't meant simply in a friendly way, it was meant as something more? I pull back a very small amount to see if she'll come forward. I'll know then. As I pull back, she follows me and kisses me. This time properly.

I can't do this! It's wrong, I'm with someone!

You're not, you're with nobody. Think about it. You're with nobody. She doesn't exist.

As slowly and as softly as I can in my clumsy state, I ease my way out of this kiss. "I'm really sorry, Julie, but I can't."

"Why? What's wrong? Are you in a relationship or something?"

"Kind of… It's complicated."

You fucking wuss. Fucking grow a pair before you ruin it for yourself. Get stuck in!

No! It's wrong. I'm not doing it.

Stop it, you fucking idiot, you're starting to cry.

I can't help it.

Julie lifts my head. "Are you alright?"

"Yeah, just pissed that's all, it's okay."

"You don't look okay. What is it? Are you married or something?"

"No. Not anymore, anyway."

"Oh, I see. I'm sorry. Is it too soon?"

I sniff, take a bit of a breath and try to laugh, but it comes out like me expelling a small amount of breath with a 'ha' sound hidden in it. "No, it's not that, Julie. It's just… complicated, that's all. I left her."

"Why?"

"Like I said. It's complicated. I'll tell you another time."

You'd better fucking not!

Will you fuck off?

"Julie, I'm sorry. You must think I'm a right fucking prick."

"Nah. I don't think you're a prick. A bid odd, maybe, but not a prick. Listen, you get yourself some sleep. I'll give you a buzz tomorrow and we'll pretend this never happened. No weirdness, no uncomfortable silences, we'll just forget it until you decide you want to talk about it. I'll walk home."

"No, let me get you a taxi."

"I'll be alright. I only live five minutes away."

She kisses me on the forehead, and gets up to leave. I watch her head towards the doorway and before she leaves, she turns around to look at me. "Remember. No weirdness, okay?"

"Okay. I promise."

She leaves.

Well, you fucked that up, didn't you?

Oh, fuck off out of my head! Jesus, why do I torture myself like this whenever I'm pissed?

Because you're a loser.

Oh, go away. I'm going to sleep.

What, so you can get back to the girl you think you're in love with?

Yeah, exactly.

But she's never going to love you back, mate.

What? Why?

Because she's mine.

What do you mean she's *yours*? Who the fuck are you?

To quote you... I'm the guy in your dreams that gets to do all the cool stuff.

PSYCHOTIC
TIM MORRIS

My heart's pounding so hard that I can feel the veins in my temples pulsating against the itchy wig I'm wearing as part of the disguise. My hands feel clammy and my stomach is in knots so big they could tie up ocean liners. This is it.

I've decided to walk, the air is ice cold and the smog from the bonfires hangs at a low level, making it uncomfortable to breathe. Every now and then a firework explodes, but it's got to be too early for the displays yet. It must just be kids setting them off. I expect.

I power towards the estate with the park on my left and there are people everywhere. Is that a good thing or a bad thing? I don't know – I don't suppose it's a bad thing. On a night like tonight, everyone that's out and about is so pre-occupied with other things that they shuffle by without a care. Rushing to a pub, or maybe the opposite end of the park, to drink, eat roast chestnuts and jacket spuds and watch firework displays.

God, that wind's fucking aggressive. As it hits me, I feel as if my face is being sand-blasted. It stings my eyes and they're streaming. I swipe at my face with my hand but instead of absorbing the tears, my leather glove spreads them across my face making me even colder. Cunt.

I pull up the collar on my trenchcoat to block the wind, dip my head, and power towards my destination with renewed vigour as I picture in my mind what I'm going to do to Tim Morris. It's going to be wonderful. It's going to be painful, messy and marvellous; I can't wait to see his fucking face.

Ok, here I am, this is his street. He's just at the bottom on the left-hand side, I've been over a few times to keep my beady little eye on him. Thus the disguise I'm donning now. Better to look like an unrecognisable twat than actually look like me. That's why I've walked here, too. No sense in getting a bus or a taxi – at least when I'm walking, people only get a glimpse of me, but if I take public transport they have the chance to look, stare, scrutinise. Anyway, I won't feel the cold on the way back; I should be on too much of a high, and it'll be dark by then, too, so I won't need to feel paranoid while I'm walking.

Right, if I've timed this correctly the car that's been loitering around, which I assume is watching him, will have gone. And... Yes... Yes, I'm clear. Nice. Another tick in the box for importance of preparation.

They'd been working shifts sometimes, but I noticed it was just the one on tonight, like it was last weekend. They rarely had full coverage on a weekend, and with this being bonfire night, too, I'm fairly sure the police have got plenty to keep themselves busy enough with without watching this tool twenty-four hours a day, seven days a week on top.

I approach his house and do another very quick mental run-through of how the start of this needs to go. I'm under no illusion that this will be easy. He's a copper, for fuck's sake; even if he's a bit rusty, he'll be more of a handful than most. And it's the getting in part that has to be the most dangerous. Once I'm in, I can do what I like, but I need to get through the door first.

I knock and wait and then something I hadn't planned for

happens; I hear him approach the door but he doesn't opened it.

"Who is it?"

Shit, I need to think fast... Do I just kick the door knowing that, as he's stood there, it'll probably knock him out? No, then the door won't close properly – too suspicious. I know. I'll give this a try.

"It's me."

"Who?"

"Me, you fucking idiot. You going to let me in?"

There's a pause, as if he's taking a second to decide whose voice it is. That's got to be a good thing. It takes no time at all to think that you can't place a voice; you know when you don't know. He's unlocking it, it's worked.

I take a glance around to check if anyone's watching, but the coast is clear. Right then, all I need to do is time this correctly and...

As soon as the door opens I spray him. He starts to cough a little and asks who I am, but then I can see the dizziness begin to take hold. I push past him, closing the door behind me, and as I stand in the hallway looking back at him, he slumps to the floor. I just need to keep him knocked out now whilst I get him where I need him. I expected him to have quite a bit more fight in him than that. He fucking stinks too, don't you? You fucking smelly old bastard. I kneel over him to look at his face. I can't believe he smells so bad – fuck! He isn't even dead yet.

I grab his feet and pull him along the hallway and into the kitchen at the back of the house. I need to get him stripped off. I suppose I ought to tie him up, too, until I've prepped what I have in store for him. I can't have him coming to whilst I'm out of reach; that would be bad.

Getting him out of the clothes isn't too bad, other than the stench. Just some pyjama bottoms and a dressing gown to take off. Straightforward. No serious problem. He can't have had a proper wash for ages. Ah well... I don't suppose it matters any more, does it?

I go into my pockets and remove some tent guy roping. It's good for my purposes because it's strong as fuck, but really light so you can carry loads of it around on you without your pockets bulging.

I roll him onto his front and tie his hands together, then his feet together, and just to make sure he's fully immobilised, I lift back his legs and tie his hands to his feet. I kick him onto his side, then rip of a large chunk of material from the bottom of his dressing gown before popping it in his mouth and securing it closed with my duct tape.

Right then, I need to find somewhere suitable. Actually, that's not the case at all, really. He's fucking heavy and I'm going to struggle as it is; I can't knacker myself out dragging his smelly arse any further than is absolutely necessary, so I'll just have to do it from here.

It's not a bad choice, really, because there's just the one window and it looks out onto a small, concrete, walled-up yard so nobody can see in. Well, it doesn't matter, anyway, because I'll just close the blinds.

There, right then. I need to find a suitable place, somewhere that will hold the weight. His ceiling is quite high. I usually have no problem in reaching up to touch a ceiling, but this room must be over nine feet high. Fucking old houses. I pull a chair out from under the dining table, solid wood, looks sturdy enough to hold me easily. I jump up and knock along the ceiling, waiting for the hollow knock to turn into the reassuring thud of a joist, somewhere strong enough to string him up.

Found it. Excellent.

I want to string him up by the arms and secure his legs to the floor, all outstretched like a human star. I've had variations on this theme kicking around in my head for years, so I bought a sex swing a long while ago because I reckoned its components would definitely be heavy-duty enough to work. I just hope this ceiling will be secure enough.

I jump down and give him another blast of the spray, then grab a ceiling hook belonging to the sex swing from my pocket. I pop it in my mouth and climb up onto the chair to get it into the ceiling.

There we go. Just need to pop a second one over there... and... sorted.

I'll just give him another quick blast, I suppose. It wasn't long since the last one, but this next bit isn't going to be easy and buying myself a couple of extra minutes could be worth its weight in gold.

I release the rope connecting his feet to his hands and look down at him slumped there on the floor. Getting him up there is going to be fucking hard. I need to get him elevated. The dining table! That'll do; I'll pop him on there and then I don't have as far to pull him up. Excellent.

Dragging the table underneath the hooks is easy, but lifting him onto the table isn't quite so easy. It's fine lifting someone when they want to be lifted, but when they're asleep or dead, they flop around all over the fucking place.

Urgh, fucking smelly heavy cunt... There we go, now I just need to get the ropes around his arms and winch him up. And, to add to my enjoyment, I'll unblock his mouth now so I can hear him scream.

*

Well, that was a fucking right pain in the arse, I wrapped a good amount of the rope around his wrists as tightly and tidily as I could, before threading the free end through the loop, but when I pulled to try and lift him up this way, he was really heavy.

The second arm, his right, was much easier and once I'd secured the ropes, I looked at him. Raised to his knees on his dining room table, arms outstretched upwards and head flopped down to his chest, he looked like a Jesus tribute act that'd had his cross nicked. I just needed to remove the table and hope everything would support his full weight.

I tried dragging the table from under him, but it was just too heavy with him being on top of it, so I tipped him off then moved the table to the other side of the kitchen. The ropes and hoops had secured him and he was now hanging with his arms outstretched about two feet off the floor. It wasn't really high enough but it would definitely work.

I waited for him to come around again and sprayed him once more because I didn't fancy being booted in the face by him whilst trying to do his legs. His legs themselves were simple to secure, but screwing the supports into a concrete floor took a while.

But he's exactly where I need him now. There he is, like a floating, hairy, overweight, old, naked, smelly mannequin. He's starting to come around a bit, he's making grumbly noises and he's trying to move. I'll give him a couple of minutes to come round before I get properly started. I want to make sure I've got his full attention.

I give him a little slap around the chops to help him come to. "Wake up!" Another slap. "Come on, you smelly old fucker, wake up."

His head's upright and the look on his face is a picture.

"W-W-What, what the fuck? What's going on?" He's trying to wriggle his arms and legs but I've got him pulled so tight that his efforts are just resulting in twitches. Like a fish. He looks at me and blurts, "Who the fuck are you? What do you want?"

Fair questions, I see no need or point to lying. "I'm Jeremy Wilkinson and I want to torture you and then kill you."

"Let me go. Do you know who I am? You're making a big mistake."

"Nope. I think you'll find that I know exactly what I'm doing and exactly who you are."

"Listen, what do you want? Money? I can get you money."

"I don't care about money, Tim. I get off on torturing and killing people that deserve to die and I've been waiting for today for quite some time. I'm going to enjoy this one. I've been really looking forward to it."

"Please let me go."

"Fuck off, do you know how long it took me to get you strung up there?"

I delve into my inside pocket which is long and deep and might have been designed to conceal a brolly or something. I pull out the ceramic hair-curling tongs I've brought to torture him with and place them on the table to the side of him, then plug them in.

He keeps wittering on, but it's boring. I can't be arsed replying any more.

Actually scratch that – he's just said something interesting. "What? " I ask.

"It's you, isn't it?" His eyes are wide, as if some kind of penny has dropped.

"What do you mean?"

"Julie Newton, John Goodchild. It's you who killed them. Scott was right."

I clap slowly. "Well done. Fucking hell, you were on to me then, were you?"

"Not really, it was just a theory. Listen, let me go, I'll give you time to get away, somewhere safe."

"I am safe, you thick cunt. I'm going to kill you. You were supposed to be my last, but it sounds like I might need to kill this Scott, too. What's his surname?"

"I'm not telling you – fuck off!"

"Oh, come on now, there's no need for this to get nasty, is there?" I take the now nicely hot tongs and press them lightly against his right nipple. He screams. "Dempsey. It's Dempsey."

Fucking hell, it's like all my Christmases have come at once. This couldn't have turned out any better if I'd planned it. "Scott Dempsey. There's a coincidence. He's my long-term project. I'll tell him how little it took for you to give his full name up."

"What do you mean, long-term project?"

"Well, you know my, erm... What is it? M.O., they call it on American films. My method. A nice dollop of torture with a sprinkling of death."

"Yes."

"Well, unbeknown to Scott Dempsey I've been torturing him for over a year. The cunt."

"What?"

"Yes. I'm trying to drive him insane. I don't know how effective I'm being, because I don't have time to watch him constantly, but it doesn't matter anyway now. I'm going to have to kill him."

"What's he ever done to you?"

"It's not what he did to me. Anyway, that's not important. What is important is what I'm going to do to you and why."

More pleading... Boring. Boring. "Tim! Tim, *ssshhh*. Do you know who my first kill was?"

He's crying, talking to me through sniffles. "Who?"

"Jack Wilkinson who used to have Jacko's Caff."

"That was you?"

"Yes, that was me. I killed him because when I was a kid he abused me. And I'm killing you not because of the drugs or any of that bollocks, but because you flogged kids to peados."

He's trying to justify it but I'm not listening again. I grab the tongs and hold them out in front of him. "So here's what I'm going to do, Tim. I'm going to shove these red hot tongs up your arse as hard as I fucking can, so that you grasp some kind of idea about what these kids went through, before I blow your fucking head clean off with a point-blank shot from my gun."

More pleading and crying. I take the tongs and ram them hard up his arse and he screams in agony. I grab a cloth from the sink and ram it in his mouth to shut him up, before pulling out the tongs and jolting them full force back in again. Stifled whimpers please me as I increase the speed and severity of the action. Faster and faster. Harder and harder.

My arm aches, so I switch to my left and, with one final almighty jolt, I leave them wedged deep inside him and take a seat on the table to watch what happens.

*

So I've been sitting here for a while now watching him, and I don't know what I expected. I suppose I had optimistic visions of it melting him from the inside, perhaps dissolving the contents of his bowels into his bloodstream and slowly poisoning him whilst filthy-looking, awful-smelling discharge dripped from his body, but that's not how it's happening.

It appears to be cooking him. He's been trying to scream non-stop now for at least twenty minutes and I can see that his thighs appear to have cooked and it's spreading. It's a little more boring than I'd anticipated, there's no discharge, although he has pissed himself, but I'm impressed with the pain he's going through and how long it could last. It's almost a shame to shoot him.

Yes, I haven't changed my mind on that one. I'm definitely shooting him – in fact, fuck it. There's enough fireworks going off now, I reckon. I'm going to do it.

Okay, what do I need? They can link a gun back to someone by the powder given off when the gun discharges the bullet. That powder will end up all over this room, the gun, and all over me. I wish he'd pipe the fuck down so that I can concentrate.

Think, think, think… If I make sure I get rid of these clothes properly, then there's no reason for me to end up with anything covered in the powder. Or I get rid of the gun. Yeah, I need to get rid of the gun, that's all. Boil the fucker first and lift it straight into a bin bag with some pliers, then get rid of it somewhere. And get rid of the bullets. Then there's the matter of silencing it a bit. The fireworks will cover up a bang, but I don't know exactly how loud a bang it'll create and it's better to be safe than sorry. I think I saw someone fire into a pillow to silence a gun once. I can't believe I'd not thought about all this and tried a few different ideas first.

What if this gun's been used for some other crime? What if they link the gunshot fired here to some random incident somewhere else? It'll be even worse if they've caught someone for that incident and want to find out where the gun went. Fucking hell, what a mess. I know, I know what I'll do. I'll get my beard and wig and stuff back on and go and knock next door. No, no, no, that won't do, it looks too crap close up. Fuck!

Oh my God, of all the things I've done, it's turning out to be something as simple as shooting someone that's proving the most difficult. Right, fuck it! I'm just going to do it. I'm going to put the nozzle to his ear, pull the trigger and watch what happens, then casually leave, via the back door obviously, and walk back to town. I'll take the route through the park and when nobody's looking, I'll remove the beard and wig, then continue walking. I'll get to town, get in a cab and go home.

What about my clothing? Even without the beard and stuff my clothes could link me back. I'm glad I'm fucking quitting, because this just isn't what it was cracked up to be anymore.

Fuck it, fuck it. Here I go. The gun is right at his ear, he's trying to scream, trying so hard that his face has gone a bluey colour like he's having trouble breathing. I take a step back and take a breath, focus on his ear, and squeeze the trigger.

BANG!

Wow! Oh, that feels good, that feels fucking amazing, the noise ringing in my ears is incredible and in the split second it took me to blink with the shock of the shot, his body jolted towards me from the force of the other side of his head blowing clean off. The force must have been immense because it's pulled his left arm loose. The entry point in his left ear is clean, but the opposite side of his head is a fucking mess; there's blood, bone and flaps of skin all over the place, it's pretty much been blown clean off. Ha! Ha, ha! Over the other side of the kitchen, his ear is clinging like a limpet to a flowery ceramic fruit bowl! As I close my eyes, I can almost picture it all in slow motion. The side of his head exploding and his ear propelling across the room surrounded by a thousand tiny bits of brain, thrusting forward and splatting satisfyingly onto the fruit bowl. Fucking mint.

His body is spasming. What the fuck is going on? Jesus! The bullet just came out of his fucking shoulder! What the fuck was that all about? It must have been ricocheting around his insides. Wow! Shooting people is fucking brilliant. Why have I never done that before? Right, I need to get out of here.

ESCAPING
PIECING IT ALL TOGETHER

So, nobody has been to see me in the whole time I've been in here, other than that cop and that reporter. I take it I'm not so popular then, eh? Who am I? I mean, I know who I really am, but who did I end up as? What have I fucking done? Oh God, it might be better if I just never find out, but where will I be then?

I still can't move my legs properly. It's so strange because I feel like they're moving, kind of like the signals that I'm sending to them are registering in my brain, but there's no physical response from them. My arms are the same. I managed to move my finger slightly after an hour or so of concentrating, but even then I can't be sure whether it was me actually moving it, or just some well-timed involuntary twitch.

I have a physio who comes in to see me, and a counsellor. They're both okay but it'd be nice to have someone here that cared. Surely there must be someone, somewhere who's missing me? Who loves me, even. I must be at least in my early thirties.

Nadia! Nadia loves me! God! I remember...

*

After I'd got back from my travels, I didn't return to Holme Bridge, I went back down south to Bracknell. I'd kept in touch with Doreen the whole time and I went back to see her. She had her own place and said I could crash there until I found something more permanent. I'd never really had a 'proper' job, but she was doing telesales at this place that sold glue and stuff and she got me a job.

I really enjoyed it, too. It was such a laugh; a massive, rowdy room full of people in their late teens and early twenties all earning alright money from chin-wagging to customers, making up special offers and stuff like that. They used to run competitions all the time with cash prizes for the most sales, the most new accounts opened, and all that kind of thing, so it wasn't long before I could afford to put a deposit down on a flat of my own.

At work, we were all like a little family. We worked together through the day and, on a night, we went out and got pissed together. I don't think there was anybody in there who I didn't like. There was one person in particular who I did like though; Nadia. She was stunningly beautiful. I know that sounds clichéd, but I mean it. She wasn't just pretty or good-looking, she was absolutely fucking perfect. She had Asian roots, her family came from Afghanistan, she had a perfect, soft, brown complexion, her skin was immaculate, she had massive brown eyes and a really nice gentle manner. She was a complete contrast to the bolshie, cheeky arrogance that coated the exterior of everyone else – including me. Yes, she was perfect. In every way.

She kept herself to herself most of the time and I often tried to engage her in conversation at lunch time or on fag breaks, but she was so shy. That just attracted me to her even more. She was an absolute world away from the countless good-time holiday girls I'd bedded whilst I was away, and found her absolutely captivating.

I'd asked her out a few times and she'd always declined, but on one particular day she was looking really pissed off so I went to speak to her. She wasn't opening up, but I offered to go for a walk with her at lunchtime and she accepted. The building was by the side of a lake and we walked around it. She opened up to me then, telling me that her family wanted her to marry one of her cousins. They were really putting pressure on her and she didn't want to marry someone she didn't love.

I didn't bother offering much in the way of opinions as I really didn't see the point. I know from experience that sympathy and empathy and "Oh, I know how you feel", and "Oh that must be awful", are a waste of time, so I offered her another alternative; an ear. I just simply listened.

Her family sounded really old-fashioned. They'd wanted the promise of a better life over here but weren't willing to adapt to their surroundings. Her father had come over shortly after the second world war to work here and, to be fair to him, he worked like a dog to be able to afford a base to bring over her mother and her two older brothers. He'd continued to work tirelessly to support them and over the years the size of the family had grown, but Nadia's mother never got the girl she'd always wanted. Apparently, her father was pleased with this but later in life, when her mother was well into her late forties, she fell pregnant with Nadia.

Unfortunately, her mother died during what turned out to be a very difficult childbirth and since then, her father and brothers hadn't really known what to do with her. She was treated as an outcast, made to cook and clean for them as she got older, and her father made no secret of the fact that he held her responsible for the death of her mother. She had little in the way of friends through school, mainly due to the fearsome reputation of her brothers, and it wasn't until she reached eighteen that she finally stood up to them and told them she was getting a job and standing on her own two feet.

She told me that all she'd ever wanted to be was normal and I knew exactly how she felt. After a few weeks of us hanging out together at lunchtimes, I told her that I'd never known my mother. I told her about my father being in prison, that I'd not seen him for God knows how many years and didn't care if I never saw him again. Within a few weeks, I confessed to the abuse that I'd had to endure as a child, and the knock-on effect it had had when I finally did find a family that I truly felt connected with.

I remember the feeling after I'd told her, like someone had lifted a weight from me, like I'd finally exorcised some of the demons that had been plaguing me and following me around all my life. I thanked her. I know it sounds a bit cheesy, but it was a nice moment. We connected, two people from such opposing backgrounds, brought up in an entirely different way that was, for all intents and purposes, exactly the same. We were kindred spirits; no, we were soulmates. Jimbob and Doreen were excellent friends and I loved them both, but I loved them in a different way. I suppose for most people it's easy to categorise these types of love and distinguish between them, but it wasn't for me. I knew I loved Jimbob and Doreen but I had no inclination to actually be with them. I'd also had sex before and felt attraction to a girl, but this was something new, powerful, beautiful and consuming.

I remember looking at her after I'd thanked her. I hung my head and she held it up. She held my chin and stared into my eyes and said, "We're not too different, are we? You and me?"

My heart began to pound, and it was that precise moment that I fell for her. I wanted to kiss her, to hold her, to feel her close to me and smell her, but I couldn't make a move. I was frozen, petrified at the thought of doing the wrong thing and losing the one person in my life who knew all my secrets, didn't judge me, didn't care and truly understood.

I could hear my own heartbeat thumping in my ears. I tried to swallow, but it felt as if I had a boulder in my throat so I decided not to do anything. But then I thought. I remembered what that girl had said to Jimbob. You have one moment, only one moment. If you make a move too early, the relationship ends up shallow and fickle, and if you miss the moment, if you're too late, you've wondered into friendship territory and it just feels weird. This was it. This was the moment, I was sure of it. But what if I was wrong? What if I blew it?

I stuck fast to my decision not to 'do' anything, and decided to say something instead, something I'd never said to anyone. "I love you."

She let go of my chin and I hung my head again. As it hung, the pounding of my heart dropped and I went cold, but she said it back. She said it with a strange inflection to her voice, as if she'd not considered it before and had just realised herself, at that precise moment, that she felt exactly the same as I did. I looked back up at her and kissed her. A simple, soft, lingering peck followed by us embracing each other. We sat there holding each other, not saying a word, for a minute or so, and then got up to walk back to work.

I felt nervous as I reached for her hand. Would she let me hold it? Did she love me in a purely platonic way, or the same way I loved her? Would her accepting my hand make that any more clear? I didn't know, I simply reached out and she grabbed my hand, placing her fingers between mine, and she squeezed it, smiled at me and asked me if I wanted to meet her that evening. For once in my life, things were going my way.

We took things very slowly. She'd never had a boyfriend

before. There had been a couple of near misses, but her brothers had always intervened and put a stop to anything before it even started. She was adamant that she wasn't going to let that happen in this case, and insisted that we keep our relationship a secret.

It was a strain at times, a big strain. I wanted everyone to know I was with her, but she convinced me that her family would ruin things if they found out. For the first year or so, they continued to pile on the pressure of an arranged marriage and it almost broke us, as she was so upset and stressed about it all.

I decided that the best way to quash their demands would be to come clean about me. I told her I'd go with her and we'd explain together. I thought that however upset they were, they wouldn't explode if I did the right thing. It's understandable that her father wanted the best for his daughter, and that her brothers only had their sister's interests at heart, and I honestly thought that if I went and met them, they'd see that I was okay.

She finally caved in and agreed to me going to see them about fifteen months or so into our relationship, and it was one of the most uncomfortable situations I've ever been in.

She had arranged for us to see her father alone, but they were all there, the whole lot of them. She calmly explained how long we'd been seeing each other, and she also explained that I'd respected her beliefs in terms of sex before marriage, which was true. They just acted as if I wasn't there, shouting and screaming at each other in Punjabi. I tried to intervene and was abruptly cut off by her father.

"How dare you! How dare you poison my daughter's mind!"

"I've not poisoned her mind. Nadia has her own opinions and her own thoughts and I respect them, and I respect her. I would never do anything to hurt her. I love her."

There was more ranting and raving that I didn't understand, then I got turfed out of the door by the biggest two of the bothers. I remained calm. I didn't want to lose my cool and act aggressively and it took all my strength to keep a level head. I simply tried to explain that I only wanted the best for her. He threw me onto the street and I fell to the floor, then he closed the door behind him, approached me and threatened me. I was told in no uncertain terms that I'd end up in hospital if I ever even attempted to see her again, and in continuing to see her I was putting the honour of their family in jeopardy and they would protect that honour at whatever costs were necessary.

I didn't know what to do. I didn't listen to them, of course, I tried to get hold of her straight away but her phone was off. I didn't know what to do. I decided to wait until after the weekend and see her at work on the Monday, but she didn't show up. She called in sick. I kept trying to call her and even waited and watched the house, but every time one of them left, another one of them went in. I was at a loss.

Then, after a week or so, she returned to work and it was pretty obvious she'd been beaten. The swelling had gone down but her complexion was blemished. She'd lied to her brothers and hadn't told them we worked together, thank God, so they had reluctantly allowed her to return. At lunchtime, I told her we had to go, and that's exactly what we did. We just left.

We decided to head up to Holme Bridge, but we were going to stop along the way at Birmingham as she had an old friend there who she wanted to borrow some clothes and stuff from, a friend she thought could be trusted. Unfortunately for us, her hospitality was just a shield to cover the fact that she'd informed Nadia's father of where we were and was keeping us there until they arrived.

They took her and beat me to a pulp. I ended up in hospital for a couple of weeks. Broken ribs, a fractured jaw, missing teeth. They'd pushed me to the floor, surrounded me and literally took turns to kick me whilst I was down. It was actually her mate, the one that had told them where we were, who stopped them in the end and took me to hospital. They would have killed me for sure if she hadn't intervened.

Once I was out, I went straight back to Bracknell to get her. If they'd done that to me, then God only knew what they'd have done to her. I went back to work but she'd handed in her notice. I had to find her. The thing is, she was nowhere to be found. Nowhere at all.

I watched the house and never saw her come or go. I asked her friends, including the one in Birmingham. It was as if she'd simply disappeared off the face of the planet. I reported her missing to the police and she was never tracked down. Her brothers had said that she'd left the country, gone back to Afghanistan, but no records of her leaving the country were ever found.

I'll never know the truth of what happened. I'll never be able to find out the facts but it's pretty obvious they killed her. Bastards! Fucking bastards! The fucking black bastards!

JUSTICE
Making Sense Of It All

"So… Take me back to the beginning. These voices must have started from somewhere, there'll be a point when you remember first hearing them."

I'm beginning to regret this already. "It's not voices, it's just a voice. A single voice, and it's me, but it's a different me... And I'm not hearing it in the true description of the word. What I mean is, it's not an auditory hallucination, it's just in my head. I don't think anyone else can hear it or anything, I know it's just talking to me."

She crosses her legs, leans back in her chair and tips her head to the side. "Yes, of course. But when did you first hear it? You have to bear in mind that having an inner monologue is a perfectly normal thing. Some people think of it as a conscience. As you grow up and have different ideas and morals imprinted on you, your brain will deal with these by creating a rational voice or voices. In most cases they're not a bad thing. What we need to determine here is whether or not this voice is just one of those, and to do that I need to know how it started."

Well, she doesn't think I'm mad already, which I suppose is a start, but then she's not going to, I guess. She's a fucking psychologist, she charges thirty quid an hour to listen to people moaning on, it's her job. God, I hope I'm not going mad. It'd be a real inconvenience; anyway, I suppose there's only one way to find out.

"It all started about two years ago with a dream. It's a dream that's been reoccurring ever since. The dreams aren't identical, the details are always different, but the core dream is always the same. You see, what happens is I meet this girl, usually in what appear to be normal surroundings, and there's like an instant lust between us and we have an overwhelming urge to have sex, but I can never do it. There's always something stopping us. I can kiss her, I can... do... other things, but I can never actually properly have sex with her."

"When you say they usually appear to be normal surroundings, what do you actually mean?"

"There are a couple of exceptions but, for the most part, the beginning of the dream is pretty normal, it's just as it progresses that it gets more odd."

"Give me some examples."

"Okay..."

She's hung her head, what does that mean? Does she think I'm crazy? No, she's looking up at me again, she has her elbow on her knee and she's waving the pen she's holding back and forth. She's just thinking, I reckon.

This silence seems to be have been going on for quite some time. Is she pregnant-pausing me? Waiting until I add something else, enough rope to hang myself?

"I have a couple of ideas regarding your dreams, but what I'm struggling to understand here is just how exactly the dreams are linked with the voice."

I explain about what happened when I went out with Julie, the intensity of the voice, and that I was struggling with the need for cocaine.

"Ah, you didn't tell me you were addicted to drugs. That

could explain everything."

I'm not addicted to drugs! "I'm not addicted to drugs." I hope I said that calmly and quickly enough to convince her. It's the truth, after all.

"It sounds like an addiction to me. An overwhelming need. A voice in your head that you disagree with, telling you to do it."

Bollocks. "I know how it sounds, but I can assure you that I'm not, and never have been, addicted to drugs. I used to use cocaine recreationally and stopped when I joined the police force. No cold turkey, and I didn't have a problem anyway, it's not like I was selling stuff to fund my habit or anything. It was easy, I just stopped. It's only when I get really drunk that I start wanting some, and even then it's not so much the buzz of the coke that I want, it's more that I want to sober up a bit and carry on drinking."

"I'm sorry to break this to you, Scott, but you're an addict. If someone was an alcoholic or a long-term addicted smoker and they stopped, they would still have urgencies, times when they needed a drink or a cigarette, and what you're going through is no different to that. The stress of addiction can put a serious strain on you. It could easily manifest itself as a voice, and the thing to do is not trust a word it says when you're vulnerable, i.e. drunk."

If only it were that simple, "Yes, but that's just the thing. It's not just when I'm drunk. The voice has seeped over into my sober state now. The voice is here all the time, pretty much."

"Is it here now?"

No, thank fuck. "Actually no, it's not here at the moment, strangely enough. I didn't have a dream this morning, either. Not that I can remember, anyway."

"And do you think it's just coincidence that the day you decide to go get psychotherapy these things stop? I'll tell you what I think... I think you're a lot stronger than you're giving yourself credit for. Let's get to the bottom of this so we can stamp it out properly. Tell me about your life around the time when these the dreams first started. Were you happy, sad? What was happening?"

"Nothing much, really, I was in training for the police force, which is a job I'd always wanted. I was married, happily. I'd been married for about six months or so. We had a nice house. Nice lifestyle. Money was okay. Everything was fine."

"And how long had you and your wife been together before you got married?"

"Just over a year."

"That doesn't seem like a very long time to be with someone prior to marrying them. Looking back on it, do you think you got married too soon?"

"Hindsight is a marvellous thing. I suppose I did get married a bit early into the relationship, but we'd have probably still been together if I hadn't left her because of the dreams."

"And don't you think that that's a little strange? Leaving your wife for a woman who doesn't actually exist?"

"Yeah, I know it's strange. It's stupid, but in my mind I was cheating on her. I wasn't doing right by her. It was a moral decision and one I stand by."

"How was it cheating? You didn't do anything. That would be like saying masturbating was cheating. In fact, technically, masturbating would be worse because there is a sense of closure at the end. You can actually succeed."

"I don't masturbate, either. For the same reason."

"Because it would be cheating?"

"Yes. I'd be being unfaithful."

"Did you ever have any intimacy issues with your wife?"

"Not before the dreams, no."

"What about other relationship issues? Were there any underlying problems prior to the dreams starting?"

"Such as?"

"You tell me!"

"My jealousy was a problem. But more for me than for her."

"What do you mean by 'more for you'?"

"I mean, I had all the feelings of jealousy but I didn't think it was fair to burden her with it. I'd ruined every single relationship I'd had, prior to the one with my wife, through my jealousy and when I got together with her, I made a decision to not let it ruin another relationship."

"Could that be why you asked her to marry you so early into the relationship?"

"I suppose there was an element of me thinking that if she made that commitment to me, those feelings would disappear."

"And did they?"

"Not at first, no."

"So when exactly did they disappear?"

"When the dreams started."

"I want you to think about this for me. Did the dreams start prior to the jealousy fading, or after?"

"I don't know. Why?"

"What I'm trying to ascertain here is if these dreams began to manifest themselves into your life because, all of a sudden, the feelings of jealousy had suddenly stopped and you didn't know how to deal with it. Did you leave your wife because you fell in love with the woman from the dream, or did you leave your wife because you didn't feel jealous anymore? Had you been so used to having those jealous feelings that when they fell off, you thought you'd fallen out of love with your wife?"

"I don't know, in all honesty. That would make a lot of sense, I suppose, but I honestly can't say. You said something about having a theory about my dreams."

"Yes. Did you ever have a crush when you were younger?"

"Of course I did. Everyone has them."

"On who?"

"Loads of girls, film stars, singers, girls from school"

"Is there any one in particular that sticks out, something that lasted longer than the rest?"

"Yeah, Mrs Brown, my old science teacher. I fancied her like mad all the way through school."

"But you could never have her?"

"Well no, obviously."

"Does that tell you something?"

"I see."

"Exactly. I think we need to meet again but, rest assured, you're not going insane. This voice in your head will only become a problem if you allow it to be."

"What's the worst case scenario?"

"What you're doing at the moment internally is perfectly normal. You're projecting a side of yourself into this other voice. Everyone does it to a certain extent. The important thing to recognise is that the voice is you and its options and opinions are your own. It's there to play devil's advocate. It's there to help you go about your business. Stop giving it more power than it deserves. As long as you can do that, you'll be fine."

"Otherwise?"

"What can happen in extreme circumstances is that the person gives the voice too much power, so eventually, the voice slowly but surely takes over and then that person becomes psychotic. They live the part of the voice rather than the part of their own life, and in doing so, they relinquish responsibility for their actions. It's not they who are performing them, after all, it's this... alter ego. It's at that point that people become dangerous, either to others around them, or themselves. But don't worry, the very fact that you came here of your own accord offers evidence enough that you're still in control. The best advice I can give is to listen to the voice, respect its opinion and then do what you want. But don't argue with it. You'll only make it worse. Between now and next week, I want you to keep a log of all the things the voice suggests and we can have a look at it. See if we can get to the bottom of what's really bothering you. Is that okay?"

"It's fine. I have an unrelated question for you before I leave. What do you know about regression therapy?"

"For you?"

"No, it's for a witness at work who's blanked out the memories of an attack. It could help us find the assailant."

"Hypnotherapy has its place but, like counselling, it's a bit like the wild west out there."

"What do you mean?"

"It's full of cowboys. I trained for seven years to be able to sit here and do this job, but anyone can call themselves a counsellor or a hypnotherapist. It's a joke. They charge as much as I do and they've probably gone on a two-day course. It's pretty immoral, in my opinion. Particularly the religious counsellors."

"What do you mean?"

"I mean, they advertise as counsellors, sit and listen to people's problems for a few sessions, and then start preaching to them. Converting them. It's disgusting. They prey on the weak. That Asian guy who was murdered a few years back used to do it. Hypnotherapy is the same. If your victim is going to be regressed to a point where the victim was really distressed, it could do untold damage to their mental health if it isn't handled properly. I can't recommend anyone for you, I'm afraid. I try to stay away from all that, but all I would suggest is that you choose carefully. And don't expect too much."

"Okay, thanks."

"Pleasure, see you next week. And don't forget the log."

*

Well, it would appear that I am perfectly sane, after all. Save for a few jealousy and insecurity issues, and the fact that I've clearly still not got over a crush that I had on my teacher fifteen years ago, I don't masturbate, and I have a severe cocaine addiction. Besides all that, I'm normal. I don't know whether I should be happy or sad about it. It's probably for the best if I don't mention any of this to Julie. I've got to go interview Jonathan Thorpe again so I'm on my way over to pick her up now. I also need to broach the subject of the regression therapy idea, I think it could work. I don't know why it didn't occur to me before, but when I opened the Yellow Pages to look up a psychotherapist, there it was, staring at me in the face, a place in the village that does hypnotherapy, counselling and acupuncture. I am a little concerned because of what the doctor just told me, but if I go into the session with Julie and flash my ID, they're unlikely to put themselves at risk by being shoddy. I'd hope so, anyway.

Here we are, number 23, she said. There she is – bloody hell, she's keen, she's standing right outside waiting for me. I give her a wave and pull the car up. As she gets in she kisses me on the cheek.

You're definitely still in there, she's gagging for you to fuck her.

"Hi. See, I told you I just lived around the corner," she says as she pulls her seatbelt on.

"Yeah, I'm surprised we've never bumped into each other before." I set off towards the hospital.

"That's because we're both always working mate. I wish the fucking insurers would hurry up and pay me for my car. It's like losing an arm. Hasn't it turned up yet?"

"No, sorry. Nothing as yet."

"Well, what will he have done with it?"

"I don't know. Burned it out, flogged it, something like that. It'll either turn up burned to a crisp, or it won't turn up at all."

"There's a lead there then, surely?"

"Eh?"

"Did anyone else's car go missing? Might be worth checking up on."

Ha! I can't believe you didn't think of that! She has a point. "Yeah, I'll check up on it when we've done this. I do have an idea, though, one that could help us catch your guy."

"Go on."

"Well, I was thinking, what's your opinion on hypnotherapy?"

"What do you mean, my opinion? I don't really have an opinion. Do you mean, do I think it's a load of old rubbish?"

"No. I was thinking about regression therapy, you know, where they put you under and take you back. There might be some details that you've blocked out that we can unearth."

"Sounds interesting. I'm up for it."

"It's not without risks though, Julie, unfortunately. It was a very traumatic thing you went through and reliving it could be extremely distressing for you. I don't want you to agree to it on a whim. Have a proper think about it for a couple of days and do what you do best."

"What?"

"Research. Find out as much as you can about it and let me

know what you want to do. I'd also like you to choose a hypnotherapist. I don't know any and I'd hate to suggest someone you didn't like."

"Oh. I thought you'd have someone who did that."

"No, no, this isn't exactly standard police procedure. I thought we could just do it off the radar. I'm happy to pay, it won't cost you anything."

"Don't be stupid. I'm not bothered about the money, I just misunderstood. I thought you were doing it through work. I already know I'm going to do it, but I think you're right about the research. It won't hurt to do some homework."

"Good."

I park the car and we head towards the hospital. Julie looks me up and down and asks me where Jonathan Thorpe's file is, but I tell her we don't need it. There's only one question we need the answer to and I'm hoping to get some glimmer of recognition from him. I don't think he was lying to us last time we met. If he thought he had something to hide, there'd be absolutely no way he'd give me his name, but I'm curious to see what he's remembered.

As we enter his room, I'm surprised to see him on his feet. He's not walking, he's balanced on a frame. He's definitely getting better; he's supporting his entire weight with his arms.

"Hello, officer," he says, lowering himself into a wheelchair.

"Hi, Jonathan. Looks like you're a little more mobile now than when we last met."

"Yeah, thank God. I was starting to panic, thought I'd end up a fucking cabbage. I still can't move my legs, though."

"And what about the old grey matter? You remembered anything that you need to tell me?"

"I've remembered a little more, but nothing that I can think will be of use to you."

"Do you want me to get to the point, or sugar-coat this?"

"Sorry?"

"Well, I did a little digging and a Jonathan Thorpe from Bracknell disappeared around six years ago."

"And… ?"

"And if that's you, you're wanted in connection with a murder."

I look at his face, but his expression shows merely shock. There's not a glimmer of him trying to cover up anything there. Not a pang of guilt or panic. Just shock.

No, look at him, you're wrong.

I'm not wrong, he doesn't know anything.

No, he didn't know anything. He's remembering, look at him, he's remembering.

You're right.

I always am.

PSYCHOTIC
ON THE PULL

So, it's about time I got myself back to normality. Other than polishing off Scott my killing and mutilation days are officially over so I'm going to have to channel my energies into something more socially acceptable. Like fucking birds.

Back to the old days. Thing is, I'm just not as good looking any more. I suppose the fact that I'm bald now instead of ginger might be a bit of an advantage, but time's taken its toll on me. I look late forties, not late thirties.

I used to go out and pull all the time, not just weekends and stuff, but all the time. I used chat lines, websites, dating agencies, pretty much anything if there was a guaranteed shag at the end of it. So here's what I reckoned; rather than go out and try to meet some bird in a pub (I am after all getting a bit long in the tooth for that now), I thought I'd go speed-dating. Should be a laugh. I get to spend three minutes each with twenty different women. I'll no doubt be a little rusty with the first few but, if I can't have secured myself a guaranteed fuck by the end of it, there's something wrong.

Don't get me wrong, I know there's more to a successful long-term relationship than the sex, but if I go straight out looking for my soulmate and end up finding her, it'll be that long since I had a shag that I'll be a flop in bed and ruin everything. I need a few practice runs to build up the old stamina again. Get the blood flow running properly through the main vein, and all that.

It'd be an absolute disaster if I were to meet a gorgeous girl who I really got on with and ended up spunking in her belly button before I'd even managed to get my cock inside her!

So, I'm all set for my speed-dating. I went out and bought myself some new smelly and a new shirt, though I didn't feel like pushing the boat out all the way to new jeans and shoes just yet. I'll save that for next time.

I'm quite nervous, actually, I can't remember the last time I actually properly spoke to a girl and I don't have the first clue what I'm going to say. I guess, as long as I don't tell them I'm an addicted killer in the process of cold turkey rehabilitation, I should be fine. As I've mentioned, before cold turkey is the only way to rehabilitate in my condition. It's not like I can wean myself off by moving onto killing animals, or just simply hurting people. It's an all or nothing addiction, unfortunately.

I'm coping pretty well though. Having said that, it has only been a few days, but I really thought that by now I'd be itching to start planning, or find another target, and I'm not at all. I think that's a good omen. They say overcoming an addiction is a simple process, inevitable almost, providing you pick the right time to do it. Like falling in love, or closing a deal, there's a window of opportunity. Sometimes it lasts a few weeks, sometimes days and other times just a few minutes, but if you can recognise it and make the right move at the right time, the right outcome is always possible. More than possible. Inevitable. It looks like I dropped lucky.

Anyway, yeah, what to say? Open questions, lots of them, that'll get me in the good books. Everyone likes to talk about themselves, especially women – they just like talking full-stop. Goes back to caveman times, that does, the old hunter-gatherer thing; men focus on one thing and women gather. Men went out to hunt and women gathered fucking berries or something. It's still true today. You get a bunch of blokes together and they'll watch footy or play cards or something, but you get a bunch of women together and they gather, they talk, talk, talk. Christ, that means they'll be asking loads of open questions of their own. I've lived a secret double life for so long, I'm fucking crap at lying when I'm asked a question outright, so I'll try and keep it as truthful as possible.

Wow, it's pretty fucking posh here, but then it needs to be for twenty-five quid a ticket. I think this is where all the footballers come for their lavish dos. Ultra modern styling and ultra clean. I really like it. I wonder where they got those chairs, big leather things with curved backs? I'll feel like I'm in the *Big Brother* fucking diary room, sat in one of those bastards, and that's all they have. Massive fuck-off *Big Brother* chairs around immaculate glass tables, not a scratch on them. Nobody's been chopping lines up on these bad boys, for sure.

Hello, only half a step through the doorway and I'm greeted by an unbelievably fit-looking bird. Dark, shiny hair – too shiny, it looks like she's combed it with an oily fish – and green eyes. She reaches out and offers me a glass of champagne. "Complimentary champagne, sir?" Her voice is husky, sexy. I take the glass and thank her. Complimentary, my fucking arse! At twenty-five quid, I want the whole fucking bottle!

She explains that on this particular event, the men all sit in one place at a single table and the women rotate every few minutes. She asks my name, then points me to a table in the far corner near the toilets. Brilliant, I hope nobody's been for a shit in there, or these women will think I stink. It seems like all the women in here have been taken to a separate room, or been told a different start time or something, because it's just blokes here. I take my seat and scan the competition. It's strange that it's not until this point that I actually start to think how sad this is. Is this sad? Am

I a loser? Who gives a fuck! I'll just turn on the charm and hopefully, by the end of this, I can at least manage to secure myself a fuck.

Urgh, this bubbly tastes like fucking fizzy piss. The least they could have done is got something good. Jesus!

Oh, here we go the fit bird's saying something.

"Okay, gentlemen, we'll be showing in the ladies in a moment. You'll see that in front of you is a pad and a pen. On the pad is a page for each of the ladies you're going to meet, and what we'd like you to do is, if there's someone you're interested in, make a note on there and hand it in to us at the end. If someone you're interested in also hands in a note saying that they're interested in you, we'll pass on their number so you can call them. Remember, this is timed and three minutes is the maximum. We'll sound a buzzer and even if you're mid-sentence, that's the end of the conversation. It's not fair on everyone else to fall behind schedule. Okay, all that's left for me to say is that we hope you enjoy the next hour or so, and good luck in meeting someone."

Right, here we go then...

*

Well, that was interesting, but I didn't take in one iota of what any of them were saying, I just found myself just trying to suss out whether they were filthy in bed or not. Did they have a shaved fanny? Or a bushy beaver? I spent my three minutes categorising each of them and ended up not being able to hand any of my pieces of paper in for the risk of being put on the fucking sex offenders' register. Here are some of my notes:

Emma
Trimmed fanny, too fit, probably a crap shag.

Jaquie
Shaved, big tits, look real. Definitely a good shag, probably doesn't swallow.

Janine
Fucking ugly, looks familiar. Think I've already fucked her, must have been crap or I'd remember.

Joyce
Old. Probably not shaved. Dry. Might do anything. Probably make an effort. Might swallow.

Ashleigh
Fat, shaved. Definitely a good shag. Prob takes it up the arse.

Debbie
Looks like a rich divorcee. Prob drives a 4 x 4, looks like she'd be a funny cunt.

Loren
Quite good-looking, a bit gothy. Not shaved. Needs a wash, probably smells.

The list goes on. I'd have liked to have had a go at that Ashleigh bird, but I can't really do anything about it now. Ah well, I live and learn. Next time, I need to concentrate. If there is a next time, that'd make it twenty-five quid twice for no guaranteed shag! I might be better off spending fifty to fuck a prostitute instead. Then again, it's not really the same, is it? Fucking a prostitute isn't like having sex, really. It's more like a really posh wank.

Thinking about wanking, I've come to realise that I may have a seriously addictive personality. Thankfully, though, I do seem to be able to transfer these addictions on a whim.

My first serious addiction was wanking. I'd fucking wank anywhere, any time, from the age of about thirteen on. I'd wanked before that, but it wasn't until I ejaculated properly that the bug bit me. I masturbated like I was out for revenge on my penis, six or seven times a day sometimes. I spent a large proportion of the time with an itchy, red-raw bell-end. My personal hygiene left a lot to be desired and as a result, I gave myself thrush quite a lot. Fucking hell. I must be the only person in history to actually give himself an STD.

I really would wank whenever the fancy took me, no matter how risky it was; probably my most risky one was when I spunked into one of the sofa cushions at fourteen years old, after wanking during the adverts in *Coronation Street* when my mum had nipped to the kitchen to make a cup of tea.

My wanking developed over the years. I'd heard there was some kind of male g-spot up a bloke's arse and spent a few years shoving all manner of stuff up there to try and reach it, but it never worked. Then I heard that if you shoved something thin inside your penis, it heightened the sensation, but that ended embarrassingly when I was rushed into the hospital after the inside of the Bic biro I'd used leaked in there. I fucked the gap between my mattress and my bed, I fucked a pint glass filled with chopped liver, at Hallowe'en I scooped a hole out of a pumpkin and fucked that; that ended in another embarrassing hospital visit as one of the seeds sliced me a bit. After that, I stuck to safer methods of getting off, like wearing tights and basques on occasion. Actually, I still do that sporadically now.

My Catholic guilt complex used to kick in now and then, and I used to have this recurring nightmare that I'd died and gone to hell. I'd wake up screaming, in a pool of my own sweat and piss, shaking with terror. My hell involved me being sat in the middle of a cinema packed with every bird I'd ever knocked one out over, and when the film started rolling it was a painfully embarrassing video of every wank I'd ever had. Urgh, it makes me fucking shiver now just thinking about it.

Seriously, I know it doesn't sound like much but I had to go for counselling. I screamed and went into a panic attack every time I went near a cinema – this stupid dream haunting me was even more traumatic to me as a teen than what my uncle had done to me as a child. I still won't go anywhere near a cinema now.

Anyway – back to the subject in hand. My addictive personality. Where was I? Oh yes... I became addicted to sex, topped up with more wanking. And when I say 'addicted', I mean *really* addicted. I had a long-term girlfriend and had sex on tap, but she soon grew tired of my constant demands. The frigid fucking bitch. I didn't think once a day was too much to ask for, but she did nothing but whinge and fucking moan. I mean, she knew what she was getting into, for fuck's sake! Why get a border collie if you only want to walk an old staffie! I spent a lot of the middle part of our relationship thinking, Jesus fucking Christ, just shut up moaning and fall asleep so I can fuck you. Then I got a bit on the side, which took the edge off, but I still wasn't satisfied. I also had serious issues regarding having sex when they were on their periods; the blood really made me gag, which seems a bit stupid now, considering the ways I've been getting my kicks ever since. I ended up with the girlfriend, the bit on the side and two fuck buddies, and to make sure I didn't have to bone any of them during rag week, I made a chart of when they were all on and only went to see them when they weren't.

Then I became addicted to killing, still accompanied by the wanking of course, although never at the same time. The sex more or less fizzled out once I'd started the killing, but it would appear now that I'm going to need it back again. Well, I suppose at least I can't get life in jail for fucking birds and knocking one out.

ESCAPING

JUST WHEN IT SEEMED THINGS COULDN'T GET ANY WORSE

As the statement rolled off his lips, I began to remember. I made my excuses. I told the truth but I made my excuses. I told him I was remembering, but asked to be left alone so that I could make sense of it all. What a fucking joke that is! There's no making sense of it. I now remember everything. I know exactly why I'm here and exactly what I've done and I'm absolutely disgusted with myself. I can't believe I let myself get so deep into the quagmire of depravity I've created, I'm a fucking murderer, a racist, a thief, and a fraud.

Once Nadia had been killed and I'd returned home from hospital, I went into a spiralling depression. I cut off contact with everyone I knew and pretty much became a hermit. I spent the bulk of my time either off my tits, or pissed out of my face, in a fucked old run-down flat on a rough estate in Bracknell. It was fucking disgusting. I was living like a junkie, selling whatever I could get my hands on to get a hold of anything that would numb the pain. Soon I had nothing left but a blanket and a table. The place was disgusting. No furniture, and a room littered with empty bottles of wine and poppers, crushed, empty cans of beer, inside-out baggies of speed and coke that had had any remnants licked and sucked away, and fucking stained patches on the lino where I'd left the vomit for fucking days on end before cleaning it up.

Everyone knew me. After a year or so, I was like the fucking village misfit. I was constantly getting involved in fights and brawls. I'd convinced myself that I was doomed, and the more I convinced myself of this fact, the more seemed to be wrong in my life. The problem peaked when I was in one of my brief spells of sobriety. It must have been just before giro day or something. I got a knock at the door and assumed it'd be one of my dealers coming around to collect money I owed. I was in that much debt, I'd lost track of who I owed what to. I answered the door with my excuses ready, and it wasn't a fucking dealer at all. It was someone far worse. It was my dad.

He looked as bad as I did, but I could see it was him. His eyes burned through me exactly like they had done when he got sent down all those years before. I froze, I was confused. I wasn't even sure if I was tripping or not, having some kind of disgusting flashback. He pushed passed me, closed the door and looked around the room.

"Look at you," he hissed, "you're a fucking disgrace!"

I turned around and watched him pacing the bedsit, lightly kicking the debris. Then he looked at me again. "This is fucking disgusting. You should be ashamed of yourself."

I couldn't believe what he was saying, after the way I'd been treated by him. Anger bubbled up inside me and I was trying so hard to suppress it that I collapsed and started having palpitations. I started to fit, maybe from the alcohol withdraw, but no doubt it was the panic at seeing my dad that had kicked it off; it certainly won't have helped. I managed to blurt out, "Well whose fault do you think that is?" amongst my spluttering and gasping.

He marched towards me and stood over me. "Fault? Don't talk to me about fucking fault, you little cunt! I've been in a fucking prison for seventeen years because of you!"

I took short breaths and tried to regain some composure but he just stood over me, looking down at me. I bet if I'd been dying, the bastard would have let me.

I decided not to take any shit off him and told him how it was. "You killed someone!"

He tensed, as if he were struggling with not kicking me or something, and blurted, "I – It was – I – I had no intention of killing her. It was a sex game! Restricting the breathing. It was an accident! She liked me to hold her throat!"

I couldn't understand. This made no sense to me. I could remember plain as day what I saw; I still can. "Fuck you!" I shouted. "Whatever you did or didn't mean to do, you still fucking killed her. I saw you!"

He began to pace around me, staring down at me, his heavy footsteps pounding around me, vibrating up through me. "You didn't know what you'd seen! You were only a child."

I glanced upwards. I'd managed to sort myself out by this point, so I sat upright and stared at him. "Exactly." I said, composed and confident. "So why the fuck were you pissed all the time? You say *I'm* disgusting, but at least it's only my life I'm fucking ruining. I don't have any responsibilities other than myself. You did. Not that you gave a flying fuck about that. Or about anything other than yourself, for that matter. You selfish fucking bastard. You got what you fucking deserved."

He stooped. I wanted to flinch but I didn't move. Inside my head, I started to lose it. I was keeping my cool outwardly, but I knew I couldn't keep it up. I hung my head. He sat down in front of me, then he reached out and once again I fought the urge to flinch, but all he did was carefully lift my chin so

I was looking him in the face. I couldn't make eye contact with him, though.

"For what it's worth, son, I'm sorry," he said. "Your mum's death hit me pretty hard."

I didn't expect that, but it didn't wash with me, either. "Sorry's not going to cut it, Dad," I said. "At least you got to know Mum. I never did. I can't remember her at all, not one little bit. I can't even remember what she fucking looked like! After you were banged up, I was passed around from pillar to post. Fucking hell, Dad, I was sexually abused!" I began sobbing violently.

He let go of my face and shouted, "So everything's my fucking fault, is it? Life's not been a barrel of roses for me, either, whacked in fucking Wakefield prison with sick scum!"

I looked at him, and this time I did look straight into his eyes. I couldn't see him well through the tears streaming uncontrollably from my eyes, but I stared. My breathing steadied and deepened and although I was still crying, I felt confidence growing inside me. The upset and anger at having him there, combined with a hangover and the comedown from a year's worth of abuse, knocked me over the edge and I got to my feet, looking down at him. I stood above him for a few seconds, then my control went and I kicked him hard, my foot striking his stomach and my knee smashing into his face.

His nose erupted and he immediately grabbed my leg and twisted it hard, really fucking hard; I almost pirouetted before collapsing on the floor. He pinned me down and sat across my chest with his shins holding down my arms. I was frantic, still crying and wriggling, struggling to get free. He was saying something to me, trying to calm me down, but it was just angering me even more. The fact that he had me pinned down caused my fury to erupt and I flicked up my legs and wrapped them around his neck, before pulling them down quickly and crashing the back of his head onto the lino.

I wriggled free, rolled him over, then punched him hard in the chin. He grabbed my arms and threw me, launching me across the room. I flew a couple of feet before crashing down onto an empty wine bottle. The pain was horrendous and fuelled my anger still further. I threw whatever I could find on the floor towards him as he approached me. He was still trying to reason with me but I was way beyond that, I had no control over myself, then, as he got within arm's reach, I smashed him with a bottle.

I found out quickly that the flip switch on my anger was hereditary, because as it made contact and the glass burst like a balloon, he flipped. He kicked me hard in the stomach and as I buckled over to cradle the pain, I felt the slice in my back caused by the wine bottle begin to tear open. This new pain immediately relieved me of feeling winded, and I scrambled to my feet and tried to run for the door, my anger giving way to self-preservation.

I didn't manage to get more than three strides away before I felt my tee-shirt tighten around my neck as he grabbed it from the back and pulled me back towards him. I was still trying to run when I felt his fist connect heavily with the back of my head. I began to fall, and spun around to grab his arm in an effort to keep my balance, but I fell anyway, as did he. He landed on top of me and we rolled and wriggled around on the floor, trying to pin each other down. I managed to get him underneath me and lifted his head before pounding it into the floor.

Suddenly, he stopped wriggling and started shaking uncontrollably. I rolled him over and could see that I'd brought his head down onto a huge shard from the bottle I'd smashed over his head earlier. The jagged piece of glass was jutting out of the back of his neck and he was making a strange gurgling noises. I can still hear it now, and see the look in his eyes. They were no longer terrifying, they were helpless – helpless soft pools of wanting; wanting me to do something to help. But I couldn't, I didn't know what to do, so I did what I've been doing ever since. I ran.

I didn't know where to go or what to do. I'd burned all my bridges. I just hoped I could find someone who'd understand. I called Jimbob first, to see if I could go and stay with him, but he was in Holland with the band. I only had one other friend left, and I'd fucked her off a while ago before all this. I just had to pray that Doreen would help me.

I knew I couldn't go to see her looking like the dishevelled mess I was. As I paced the estate, I knew that my only option was to go back to the flat and clean myself up. I showered and dried myself with a towel that probably undid all the effort I'd put into being clean, but I couldn't go and see her in the clothes I'd been wearing. They hadn't been washed for months and they stank to high heaven, so I removed my father's jeans from his corpse. I'm not proud of that; to this day it makes me feel sick when I think of it, but I had to do what I had to do. Then I rifled through his jacket pockets to find some money. He had twenty pounds. It would be enough to get me a new shirt and a bus across town. I pulled on my smelly old coat and left.

Once I'd reached the town centre, my cash bought me a pasty, some hair gel, some deodorant and a tee-shirt, with enough cash left over for a pint. My God, how I wanted a pint, to feel the cold glass touch my lips before tilting it and absorbing every minute millilitre of its glorious contents. But I knew that was the last thing I should do. I had to wait, hang around the bus station until Doreen got there to switch buses after finishing work.

As soon as she saw me, she ignored me and tried to blank

me. I had to plead with her to give me five minutes of her time, and I confessed everything. It's at times like that when you realise who your true friends actually are, and she didn't let me down. We put a plan in place and left for Holme Bridge the next day.

In retrospect, it ended up being a bad move. I had to change my name for obvious reasons, and ended up being so focused on getting out of the country that I'd do anything, anything at all, regardless of who or what was in my way, to get as far away from England as possible.

I'm ashamed of what I did. I remember what I did to Rizwan, and how I could have implicated Jerry in something that wasn't his fault. And Doreen's dead and it's my fucking fault. I hatched some stupid plan to try and get us the money and it all went wrong. Me being here now is testament to the fact that bad things happen to bad people, and now the police have obviously got me rumbled. I need to get out of here, I need to be able to walk, I need to get mobile and I need to right these wrongs.

I need to go and see Rizwan and Jerry and confess, absolve myself of everything. I'm man enough to take what they throw at me, I have to be. It's time to do again what I do best, and start running.

I lie on the bed looking down at my legs. If I can at least muster up enough strength in them to support myself, I may be able to get away with using crutches rather than having to try and flee in a wheelchair. I concentrate hard on my feet and try to curl up my toes, but I get nothing more than a twitch. I close my eyes and visualise my toes curling. I look at every detail. The angle at which the knuckle on my big toes bends, the number of creases that form in the balls of my feet, the tightening of the tendons around my ankles. I rotate the image to inspect it from every angle in the hope that building this mental blueprint will help my brain decipher the coded signals I'm sending to it. Keeping my eyes closed, I picture and count the wrinkles at the back of my ankles and the line of my calf muscles, tensed and taut, running up the back of my legs. Then I picture my feet spread, toes outstretched, and I look at the veins that criss-cross across the top of my feet.

I open my eyes, and with all my strength I curl my feet. The pain that shoots up from the bridges of my feet to my calves is incredible, but I hold it. I look down at my feet and see nothing more than a flicker, but I hold it. I close my eyes again and visualise, all the time holding my mental grip of the muscles firmly in place. I run it over in my mind again and again, and as I open my eyes I can see it's worked, my feelings aren't lying to me any more; I can see my toes curled exactly as they're supposed to be. I relax and they flip back to their natural state. A wave of relief rushes down my legs like a swishing of pins and needles, washing the pain away.

I tense again; they work, they flex. I'm trying too hard, I'm tensing with everything I have and I need them to flex without so much effort, but I don't have the time. I sit upright and lift my left leg, and as I throw it over the side of the bed, its weight and momentum pulls me off the bed and onto the floor. I manage to break the fall with my arms, and lying there, I can see the open door to my room. If anyone sees me, I'm fucked, they'll put me straight back into bed. I drag myself across the floor as quickly as I can and push the door shut. I need to get to my training poles; if I can stand up there and support myself, I can maybe try to stand on my own.

I need to think. What's the best way of getting myself over there? Should I lie down and pull myself along with my arms? No, I need to sit upright and push myself along; that way, when I get to the bars, I'll be in a good position to reach up and pull myself to my feet.

As I push, my progress keeps being hampered by my feet rubbing against, and sticking on, the tiled floor. They keep curling sideways at the knee, and I have to reverse and try again. It's frustrating, but after a mountain of effort and around five minutes, I make it across the room to the poles. I push myself as close as I can get and reach up to grab them. They're an inch or so above my head, and pulling myself to my feet seems like an impossible task. I don't know if I have the upper body strength to succeed. It would be easier if I could grab the outside of the poles, but my shoulders would get in the way of me being upright if I did it that way, so my hands are curled around the bars on the inside, with my forearms at right angles to my biceps, which will no doubt start burning when I pull myself up.

I don't go for it straight away. Instead, I visualise again, running through the exact process I'm going to need to go through to get myself up. I won't have the strength to do this twice. This is a one shot attempt and I can't afford to get it wrong.

Okay, I know what I need to do. This first part will be the most difficult. There's no sense in pushing too hard, I need to control the lift. Slowly, I pull. I feel the strain in my weakened biceps and feel my back crack with the strain between my shoulder blades, but as soon as my shoulders are level with the poles, I take the strain on my right arm as I lift my left and throw my elbow over the bar, to support myself with my armpit. I pause, gasping for breath for a brief moment before repeating the process with my right arm. I stretch out my supported arms and grasp the rail again, then I wait, panting from the effort, bracing myself for the last part. Now I don't need to lift any more. If I just pull hard, it should be enough to drag me up.

I can't do it! I have no strength left. It's taking everything I have to simply support myself. I need to muster the strength from somewhere. I can do this, I tell myself. I *can*! I close my eyes and, with every inch of power I have left in me, I pull.

Within a split second I'm upright, on the pole exactly as I would be if I were doing the physio; my legs beneath me and my arms supporting me. Now, can I stand? Can I let go of this rail and stay upright?

I jolt my arms in order to sway back a little until I feel my knees lock into position, then I lift my left arm. My legs are supporting me! I just need to hope that I can keep my balance if I let go with my right. Before I do so, I ready my left hand an inch or so above the pole, prepared to grasp it just in case, and then I slowly release my grip with the right hand.

I've done it! I'm balanced! Now I need to straighten up. This is fucking stupid. I'm stood here with my body leaning forward slightly and my arms readied to grasp, but I'm too petrified to straighten up. Jesus! I need to sort myself out. This is simple, all I need to do is straighten my back! Come on!

There! There, I've done it. Okay, that's a lot further than I've got before. I grasp the rails again and try to mimic a move with crutches. I swing forward and try to plant my locked legs below me, but as they land, they buckle, my knees unlock and I'm struggling to support myself. Right. Come on!

I swing, to lock my knees again, and that's when I see what my problem is; I need to keep them locked all the time. Once again, I visualise, seeing the tightening of my thighs this time. The lower part of my leg can swing as long as I keep my thighs tight. I can feel them tightened now, but I can't see them through the tracksuit bottoms I'm wearing so I've no idea whether or not I've just got the sensation of them being tight, or if they actually are. I mimic the crutch move again and it's a success. Perfect. Now, I just need to get to the crutches.

They're in a cupboard just at the end of my rails, so I swing along until I'm right at the end of them and the cupboard door is just within my grasp. I manage to open the door but lose my balance and crash down to the floor again, followed by the crutches, which land on me as they tumble from the open cupboard.

I need to get my breath. If this is the shape of how things are going to progress, then I'm not going to get very far at all. Probably a lot of my weakness is down to hospital food. I can't see all that processed shite being very high in nutrients. The first thing I need to do when I get out of here is get something decent to eat. But that's later. I actually need to get out of here first. Bollocks! I don't even have any fucking shoes! I'll just have to nick some; well, some trainers. I'd look even more stupid in trackie bottoms and proper shoes than I would in bare feet.

Perfect. I come out of here trying to turn over a new leaf and what's the first thing I'm going to have to do once I leave this room? Twoc some poor cunt's trainers, brilliant.

I stay down until my heartbeat returns to normal and try to suss out exactly how I'm going to manage to get upright on these crutches. I know now that I can probably walk with them, but how the fuck do I actually get myself into a position to do that without any help? And what if I fall?

I grasp the crutches under my arm and make my way to the bed; it's going to be a lot easier to do this sitting down, or rather, sitting up. Once I'm on the edge of the bed, I slide my arms through the loops and clasp the handles, then pull myself upright. It's easier than I thought it would be. Now it's time to move.

I head for the door. Pulling it open is a struggle but I manage, and then head out onto the corridor. Shit! I've no fucking idea where the exit is! And hospitals are like a maze.

It's okay, I can get through this, this is my last trial, my last penance.

"Jon... Jonathan!"

Oh bollocks, the fucking nurse, that's all I need! She's running towards me.

"Look at you. Well done, did you manage to get yourself mobile without any help?" Bless her, she looks really pleased for me.

"Yeah, I thought I'd take a walk – well, a hobble. I want to go outside; I've not felt fresh air on my face for years."

"Well, it's not all it's cracked up to be. It's freezing out there."

"Right. Erm, is there any way I could borrow a jacket and some trainers then?"

"I don't see why not. I'll go have a word with one of the patients for you. What size shoe are you?"

"A seven."

"Okay, I'll be back in a tick."

Well, that paid off. Perhaps getting out of here isn't going to be so hard after all. I can hear her shouting around, asking if anyone will let me borrow their stuff. Sounds like someone's obliged.

She comes back. "Here you are, Dave's let you borrow his. Let me give you a hand getting them on. I'll get you some socks from the back. We've only got those stupid knee-length things that stop thrombosis, but you don't want to be wearing someone else's trainers with bare feet."

Fuck me! Perhaps things really might be looking up. She comes back with those stupid socks and puts them and the trainers on for me, then she helps me on with the jacket, which is a nice, warm, hooded fleece.

"Do you want a hand getting outside?" she asks.

"No. Thanks though, but you've done enough. Plus, I'd

really like to try and do it on my own."

"Okay. Well, just keep going down here and take a left. You'll come to some lifts, press R and that'll take you to the reception lobby. You can get out from there. Now, don't go running off, will you?"

I laugh, glance down at my crutches and look back at her, then she goes. Thank fuck. I make my way down the corridor and once I'm in the lift, I rifle through the pockets of the jacket in the hope that I'll find some cash and drop lucky. I do. There's a folded up twenty pound note in the inside pocket. Jackpot!

Once in Reception, I make my way outside. She was right about the weather; it's fucking freezing, but my run of good luck continues when someone is dropped off in a taxi. I take a look around to make sure nobody is taking any notice of me, then flop into the back seat and give him Jerry's address.

"Just been discharged, have you?" asks the cabbie.

"Yeah, I'm still not perfect, though. I'll probably need you to give me a hand getting back to my feet and getting the crutches on, once we get there."

"No problem, mate. So... What did you do then?"

"Sorry?"

"What did you do? To your legs?"

"Oh, yeah, a car accident."

"You driving?"

"No, I was a passenger. He was speeding, hit a tree"

"Well, you don't look too bad considering."

"What do you mean?"

"No scratches, no pots, just some crutches. I'd say you got off lightly."

Prick. "Yes, mate. I was lucky."

As he pulls into Jerry's street, we're stopped by the police. A squad car is parked sideways on, blocking the road, and the taxi driver winds his window down as an officer approaches. I try to look cool; there's no way they'd be going to this trouble for me and, more to the point, there's no way they could know where I was going.

"Hi officer, there a problem?" the cabbie asks, an obvious but essential question.

"Yes, you can't get through to this street at the moment, all entry and exit points are blocked."

"What's going on then?"

"Not at liberty to say at this time, sir, but you'll have to back up."

As the officer leaves, the cab driver asks me what to do. I pay him and get him to let me out here. It looks like all the commotion is centred on Jerry's house. What the fuck is going on?

JUSTICE
THE TIME IS NOW

Well, credit where credit's due; that regression therapy idea of yours ended up being an absolute stroke of genius. Julie relived the entire ordeal from being in the back of his car, to being bundled into a small cellar room. The face that peered out of the top window matches perfectly what she'd described, a bald man with a drawn face, in his mid forties. He looked like a fucking ghost.

She remembered the exact route he took and remembered the driveway and garage she pulled into, but you couldn't take any chances by going in there yourself, particularly if this is the bloke who killed Tim Morris, because he's clearly armed and willing to use a gun to kill.

So here we are, waiting outside with an armed response unit. It looks like something straight out of a cop show. You must be pretty proud; this is what you've been waiting for since you joined the force. Look at this! The street is cordoned off, there are people's curtains twitching all over the place. Police cars are blocking every route in, and there's a wave of uniforms, flashing lights and stab vests washing around this otherwise quite posh little street.

In the top windows of the houses opposite, there are armed response guards with rifles aiming at each window, plus three out here, readied and aiming at the door, and some more around the back.

They're professionals, man, you should be impressed by their composure, not an ego or itchy trigger finger in sight, they're all just poised and ready. You've been here now for two hours and everyone is in place, but he's showing no sign of coming out. It's fucking cool, man. It's not like on television with hostage negotiators and all that bullshit, though. It's just a waiting game now. The thing is, the longer he leaves it, the more ready we are.

Get out of my head!

Shut the fuck up, do you really think you could have achieved all of this on your own? You need me, you were going mad before I took control. Just think how impressed Julie will be when she arrives. She should be here any minute, she's going to think you're cool as fuck, and then later you're going to go out and celebrate, have a few drinks and do what you should have done a few weeks ago – fuck her senseless. Oh yes, it'll be a perfect end to a perfect day, you'll be thankful in the morning.

Leave me alone!

Oh, fuck off, will you? You're really starting to bore me. You want to be thankful I haven't made you disappear. I'm doing this for you, you ungrateful cunt. I want you to enjoy this whilst everything's taken care of for you. Ah, here she is!

Leave her alone!

"Hi Julie, you took your time."

She looks stressed. "Yeah, I know. I was in court so my phone wasn't on. I'm well fucked off, and then those bastards kept me waiting before they let me in here, checking my ID and stuff"

"Wankers! They were told to let you straight in."

"Have I missed anything?"

"Not really, just the assembling of this pretty impressive machine you see out here ready to take him down."

"What, kill him?"

"If necessary. Hopefully not, hopefully he'll get bored and give himself up, but maybe, yeah."

"Can I ask a favour?"

"Ask away."

"Can I get a photographer up here?"

"Erm, not really. If he comes running out with a gun and your snapper's flash is going ten to the dozen, it could make a right mess of things for their line of fire. You're welcome to ring one, but he'll have to find his shot from outside the cordoned-off area, I'm afraid."

"Aw, come on!"

"No, Julie. Listen, I'll radio the guys and make sure that if any photographers other than yours turns up, they're held up longer while they're being checked, if you want. That should buy your guy some time."

"It's not a guy, it's a girl"

"Sorry, Julie, I meant 'guy' in the asexual sense. It wasn't an assumption. Jesus, what's fucking wrong with you today?"

"Oh, I'm sorry, really sorry. I'm just fucked off because I've missed everything, that's all."

"You haven't missed anything yet. It starts now, everyone's in place. Plus, in two hours' time, when we're all still standing here bored shitless ,you'll probably be grateful you missed the beginning."

You get the photographer's name and radio through to fulfil your promise. Jesus, she's fucking arsey today. You wouldn't have bothered calling her, if you'd known that all she was going to do was fucking complain. This is the moment you've both been waiting for.

We need to get things moving along more quickly. Can't we just throw a fucking smoke bomb or some tear gas in there, or something? Maybe even just fire a couple of warning shots!

That's too dangerous, though, on a street like this; we can't afford a single stray bullet going anywhere if that maniac gets freaked and runs out in a frenzy, all guns blazing. It's wrong to put the public in danger, and unfortunately, these poor fuckers with the guns will end up being the ones putting their lives at risk, because sooner or later they're going to have to go in and get him. They've been to the house two doors up to get an idea of the floor plan, and nosed around the neighbours to get as much information as possible. It would seem that this guy doesn't just look like a ghost, he pretty much is one; very rarely comes and goes, very few visitors, hardly makes any noise.

We called his work hoping to get hold of him there, but he spends most of his time out on the road, apparently. It was more luck than anything else when you drove past just by chance and saw him at the window. He must have been skiving. Well, it'll serve him fucking right now, won't it?

You can see Julie's getting bored with this already and she's only been here a half hour. Thankfully, the armed response team are readying themselves to enter, so we should finally see a bit of action. What will you do then? Have you thought about that? What'll be next? Things look good for your career, but surely anything else will be a little bit of an anti-climax after all this? It's a good job I'm here to help you out.

Wow, look at them! It's getting a bit more movie like now. There are three of them at the door, one positioned next to it with his back against the wall and the other two facing it, and the same is happening around the back, apparently. They're shouting through the door, telling him he has one last chance to come out.

Nothing. He's obviously hiding in there somewhere. One of the other armed response crew has brought over a small ram. Here goes... They're in!

PSYCOTIC ESCAPING JUSTICE
THE END

As Jonathan Thorpe hears the shots, his mind is still awash with questions. Questions such as, why were the police outside Jerry's house? Was it still Jerry's house after all this time? If it was, have they just killed him? Has he killed one of them? He counted at least three shots. That would show signs that there was some kind of attack or retaliation, as the police wouldn't need three shots without being provoked, surely? Two at the most; a warning shot and then a real one. Ideally, no shot at all.

He's fully aware of how at risk he is. The fact that he's missing will have been reported by now but clearly the police have bigger fish to fry than him at the moment. Plus, he needs to know what's going on.

He sees the paramedics rush from the ambulance and into the house, there are six of them, something bad definitely has to have happened, more than one person must have taken a bullet; it doesn't take six of them to sort out one casualty.

At the core of all this commotion. Detective Inspector Scott Dempsey and Julie Newton rush into the house, hot on the heels of the paramedics. As they enter, the voice in Scott's head is surprised at how 'normal' the house appears; it's well decorated and tidy. It almost seems to have a feminine touch, like a show house or something plucked straight out of an advertisement in *Yorkshire Life*. That is, until he reaches the living room, where a spray of blood and brain swipes across the back wall, seemingly propelled from the head of the body neatly fitting Julie's description, that lies limp and lifeless on the floor. Opposite him, gasping for breath, is the armed response officer who took an almost point blank shot to the chest from him. His vest has saved his life but the shot has still left him in absolute agony. Thankfully, the paramedics have the situation under control and quickly remove the vest. As the pressure is released from his chest, he lets out a huge moan, coughing and gasping, as three of them surround him and attend to him.

Jonathan's anxiety is beginning to take over and, as cameras and crowds begin to surround the crime scene, he realises he needs to get out of there as quickly as he can. He's torn between his curiosity, the needing to know what's happened, and the reality of his situation.

His thoughts turn to Rizwan. He knows it's going to be a difficult confrontation, but he has demons to exorcise and his soul to cleanse, and apologising and explaining to Rizwan is a major part of that plan. Plus, in the situation he's in, he has nowhere else to go and nobody else to turn to. He stumps away from the hectic scene, forcing his legs to keep swinging and his armpits to keep resting on the painfully hard crutches, and hopes that, in the time he's been incapacitated, Rizwan hasn't moved house. If only he had a nice, speedy electric wheelchair…

Meanwhile, in a small but classy bar on the outskirts of the village, everyone's attention has turned to the plasma screen on the wall bringing the live feed of the activity surrounding Jeremy Wilkinson's house.

The news reporter's monotone drones narrate the blurred and shaky camera images, "….and after a three-hour stand-off, armed police broke into the house to confront the suspect. Although no official name has been released, we are aware that the house belongs to a Mr Jeremy Wilkinson. Nobody knows at this time what the reason for the stand-off has been. According to our sources on the scene, three shots were fired and we have reports that there has been a fatality to the assailant, presumably Mr Wilkinson, and an injury to one of the officers…."

The wobbly camera zooms in on a dead body being carried out on a stretcher, before a large hand, presumably that of a police officer, covers the lens. Jerry Wilkinson slowly leaves the bar, hoping he's gone unnoticed, and once outside he calmly lifts his collar, puts his head down and powers towards his car.

He turns the corner into a small alley leading to the car park. Halfway down, he breaks into a panic as worry and frustration overcome him, and he has to stop himself from vomiting. He realises that they've finally figured out who he really is. He knows that he's now living on borrowed time and a fury is burning inside him as the images of the body on the stretcher flash through his brain. He's distraught and upset that he's just seen the body of his guinea-pig being carried out of his house by paramedics, with half his head blown off.

*

Jonathan, his arms aching painfully from his efforts with the crutches, approaches Rizwan's door and knocks. His nerves are twitching but he knows what he has to do. As he sees Rizwan opening the door, his reaction is a twisted combination of relief and dread.

"Riz, We need to talk," he says to a shocked-looking former friend.

*

Jerry pulls himself to his feet, then his efforts to control his urgent desire to vomit fail him, and he coughs and splutters burning bile all over the ground. He takes a breath and catches control again before continuing on towards his car. But, as he approaches it, he realises that driving that is the last thing he should be doing. He knows full well that it's only a matter of time before the police realise that the person they've killed isn't him. He begins to sob at the thought of his poor guinea pig. After everything they'd been through together, they were so close to coming out the other end now he's been killed.

His guinea pig was originally intended to be his third kill. Once he'd bought the pets to experiment with their toxins, what better way to experiment on them than by using a doctor who was hated by animal rights campaigners because of his work related to animal testing? Dr Alan Wake was a perfect target for Jeremy. He'd definitely done wrong and there was a huge number of potential suspects and the punishment would fit the crime. The thing was, Jerry had spent so long trying out the toxins on Dr Wake that, after months of being mildly to moderately poisoned and knocked out, he'd decided he wanted to see the effects of what Jerry had in mind for his victims, too. He willingly became Jerry's assistant. Stockholm Syndrome had kicked in big-time and eventually, he helped with the planning and preparing of most of the concoctions – always allowing Jerry to test them on him first, of course. Craving it, in fact, as if he got a kick from it – which, in some indescribable way, he did. He even helped and advised Jerry on the best way to carry out some of his more ambitious and intricate plans.

Jerry thinks back to the news report and remembers seeing Julie Newton and that cunt policeman. What the fuck were they doing together? Anger and rage bubbles inside him, which combines with the panic and flips a switch in his brain. All control is lost now. The demons inside him are no longer slaves to his fantasies, and they've decided for him that at this point, if he's going down anyway, he's taking those two bastards with him.

He has to do some quick thinking, as he's fully aware that he doesn't have the usual luxury of time or his guinea pig and toxins to help him. He's going to have to do this one alone, and it needs to be a good one. Yes, he thinks, a good organic couple of kills, no daft gimmicks, no games, no concoctions, nothing but cold, hard torture and an immaculately painful demise. Perhaps that's what had been missing from his last few, perhaps they were too clinical, too organised. Yes… Yes he thinks that must have been it! All that time spent choosing, planning and preparing had been diluting the buzz. Well, not this time. This time he'd get two for the price of one, torture them for hours, make them die from the pain, make one watch the other first, get the biggest buzz he's ever known and then finish it by killing himself. He knows he can't go to prison, he isn't built for it. Nope, he's going to go out with a bang!

*

Over at Rizwan's house, Jonathan can barely believe his ears at the explanations and revelations he's just been confronted with, by a man he knew as someone entirely different.

"Well," Rizwan says as he relaxes back into his chair, "I don't really know what to say… I mean, I don't know what you want me to do. But, to quash your concerns, no. No, I'm not mad at you, not at all. I suppose, if you hadn't reported me, I'd have ended up being the driver in that getaway and I'd have been in a lot worse position than I am currently, and as far as Jerry goes, I think we need to find him. But don't feel bad about reporting me; after all, it was once I was released from prison that I bucked up my ideas.

"I can understand completely your issues surrounding race, and it sounds as if your fiancée could possibly have been honour-killed, but there's something you need to understand about them. Honour killings aren't anything to do with our religion, they're to do with small-mindedness and people bringing the culture of small eastern villages into a western civilised society, and those people are fucking scum. England has given me an opportunity and a life that I'd never have had if I'd been born in Pakistan and I respect that. In fact, I'd go so far as to say that the bulk of the Pakistani community around here respect that. It's just a shame that there are a few, mainly the older families, that are clinging onto an Eastern way of life that simply doesn't work in our society. And, to be honest, they're as racist and responsible for fuelling racism as any skinhead or Nazi.

"I'm glad you've admitted to me that you were racist and I'm glad you've realised you were wrong, because I reckon we're not far off it going all together. You have to bear in mind that the bulk of the small-mindedness comes from people who weren't born here, and now most of us have been, so when we come to have families of our own they'll be brought up differently.

"I'm not saying that we'll forget our religion, not by any means, and I know I've been far from an upstanding Muslim in the past, with the drink and drugs and what have you, but I love my religion. That doesn't mean I'm going to force it down anyone else's throat, though. I think you had a good reason for being racist, but don't ever think that what they did was done on religious grounds, because nowhere in my religion does it say it's okay to kill someone. And, like I said, it's just a shame some of our community don't realise how well off they are here and how good Britain has been to them. I mean, talk about double standards. You look around my neighbourhood and there's a mosque, a halal butcher, an Asian DVD rental place... Can you imagine if you wanted to live in Pakistan and you went over, brought a load of your mates over with you and opened up a fucking church, a pub and a bacon buttie shop? They'd fucking kill you! Trust me, their racism and double standards anger me just as much as anyone else. They're all the same; they're racist for one reason and one reason only. Ignorance. They've probably never really known, and I mean known, not met, anyone that they're actually prejudiced against, that has prompted them to make a judgement. They're fucking idiots, but their numbers get smaller all the time. Hopefully, by the time the next generation comes around, they'll have pretty much disappeared all together"

Jonathan strokes his chin in thought. He knows Rizwan is speaking sense. "Do you know something. Riz?"

"What's that?"

"Well, firstly you're right, but secondly, I think this is the first time I've ever sat down and had a real conversation with you."

"Of course it is. You're not who you were claiming to be, are you?"

"Well, no, but that aside, we never actually spoke, did we?"

Rizwan giggles to himself. "Well, that's because I hated gay people."

Jonathan joins in the laugh, "Now, there's some double standards, bearing everything you've just said in mind."

"I don't know. I was guilty of the same thing I was just accusing other people of. I still don't think it's natural, but to each their own, eh? Plus, for each gay bloke there's a girl going spare!"

"I suppose. So, do you want to go for a pint whilst we figure out what to do about Jerry? You'll have to drive me there, though. I don't think I can walk one more fucking step."

"I don't drink any more, not since I got banged up."

"Why?"

"I took it as a wake-up call, decided to pull my head out of my arse and fuck off the drink and drugs. Jesus, I'm even having an arranged marriage."

"Fuck off! When?"

"Next month."

"What? And you're okay with that?"

"Yeah, it was my idea. I've met her and everything, she seems really nice. She seems to like me well enough, too, so we'll see what happens."

"Fucking hell, it's not just me that's changed, you're a different person."

"A better person, mate. It seems like you are, too."

"Yeah, well. If we're not going to the pub, do you mind doing me a favour?"

"What's that?"

"Put the kettle on. I'm fucking parched."

*

Inside the police station, Scott's in Jim Kaney's office. However, the conversation they're having this time is worlds away from the one Jim had had with him in the interrogation room all those weeks ago.

"Well, Scott I have to hand it to you, you did a really good job there." His boss walks over to the door, closes it and pulls the blinds to protect their privacy. He then heads back to his desk, picking up a couple of small plastic cups from his water cooler on the way past. Then he takes his seat, slides open his drawer and pulls out a small bottle of Scotch. It's a rather expensive Scottish Malt, not that Scott notices.

As Jim pours himself a glass, the voice inside Scott's head

begins to laugh; that nice little nip of whisky will keep his power levels up and keep Scott away for at least long enough for him to get to the boozer.

"Thanks, boss," says the voice, as Scott downs the whisky in one.

"Steady on, Scott, that's a very nice malt. I only crack it out on very special occasions."

"Sorry, boss, I just needed that, that's all."

Jim smiles, "Yeah, I suppose you did. I'll tell you what, mate, why don't you get yourself off, eh? Go and have a few pints. There's fuck all else you can do around here. The body needs identifying, although that's a foregone conclusion, and there's a load of paperwork to do, but you can't finish it until we have the reports in from the other officers, anyway. You get off, you've earned it. And I'll see you tomorrow."

"Nice one. Thanks, boss."

Scott stands up and the voice in his head can't wait to get to the evidence room to swipe some cocaine. And then get to the pub for a few pints with Julie. And then back to hers to fuck her fucking brains out.

*

Rizwan's and Jonathan's jaws hit the floor as they see the news report and realise that it was Jerry the police were after, and they've mistakenly killed the wrong man.

"Jesus fucking Christ, Tarquin, what are we going to do?" asks Rizwan

"It's Jonathan."

"Huh?"

"It's Jonathan."

"Yeah, whatever. What do we do? The police obviously want Jerry for something pretty serious."

"Yeah, I suppose so. But I don't know what to do. They're probably after me as well."

"Whose side are we on here?" Rizwan switches off the TV to make sure he's got Jonathan's attention, before asking again, "Whose side are we on?"

"What do you mean?" asks Jon, puzzled.

"I mean, do we tell the police they've got the wrong guy, or try to find Jerry and warn him that they're after him?"

"I don't know; it depends on what he's done I suppose."

"Yeah but that's the thing. We don't know what he's fucking done, do we? The news report didn't say. Jesus! It didn't even speculate." As the words leave his mouth, Rizwan silently hopes that Jonathan wants to help Jerry like he does. After all, while Jonathan's been in a coma, Rizwan and Jerry have maintained contact. Riz's uncertainty over what Jerry could have done gives way to a confidence that it can't be that bad. Surely, if it was so bad, Jerry would have given something away, or said something? Or asked for help, even?

"Well, there's one thing that's for damn sure," says Jonathan, "and that's that I can't go anywhere near a fucking police station."

Rizwan masks his relief, "Of course. Well you never know this could work out well for you."

"How?"

"Well, Jerry's going to need to get away, you need to get away. You've got no money and he's fucking loaded."

Jonathan ponders silently for a moment before realising that this idea of Rizwan's could be the perfect solution to his problem. "How are we going to find him, though?" he asks.

"I don't know mate. No idea whatsoever."

*

Jerry strides on through the horrendous icy wind blasting hard towards him as he powers towards Holme Bridge. He has no idea of how to find Julie and Scott. The rational part of his brain is closed off, his only function now is to kill them both, and anyone else that stands in his way. He barely notices the cut in his thigh and the blood pouring down the back of his leg from the machete that he just purchased at the pawn shop, which is hidden down the inside of his trousers, and he's oblivious to the fact that he's walking strangely due to not being able to bend his arm because of the recently purchased cricket bat down his sleeve.

He's aware that he has the luxury of a little bit of time, as it will obviously take the police a few hours at least to realise that they've killed the wrong man. He'll just have to take the gamble, head into the belly of the beast. Straight into the police station. If anybody rumbles him, he'll just have to go down fighting.

*

Jonathan struggles to his feet and secures his balance with the crutches. He is tired, bone weary, and his long disused muscles and tendons are shrieking in protest. "Listen, you don't need to drink. I'll buy you a glass of pop or something, but I've not had a fucking pint for years. Please can we go to the pub so I can have a beer and a smoke?"

"Hee-hee, you can't have a smoke. It's been banned."

"You're fucking joking, aren't you? You mean, I can't have a cig?"

"You can have a cig, just not in the pub. Outside."

"Oh, thank fuck for that."

Rizwan leaves the room briefly and re-enters after a minute or so with his jacket on, ready to go. "Come on, then."

*

Scott is locked into a small cubicle in the toilets of the Dog and Duck, emptying out a liberal amount of cocaine onto the porcelain lid of the toilet cistern.

This'll sort you out, Scottie boy… Get some of this fired up your nose and then we'll get some of that (grabbing cock) *fired up Julie-fucking-Newton.*

No! No, I won't let you take it.

Oh, you don't have much choice, mate.

Yes, I do! Yes! Do!

As Scott grabs hold of his mind, he immediately swipes the coke off the cistern and into the bog.

You cunt. After everything I've done for you, this is the gratitude I'm shown?

Get out of my head!

Get me out you fucking loser!

As the voice grabs Scott again, it doesn't waste any time pissing about with tipping out the coke on to the cistern this time, and Scott ends up with his nose in the bag, inhaling an obscene amount of pretty much pure cocaine. As the voice settles in, Scott laughs hysterically.

There you go… You're fucked now aren't you? There'll be no getting rid of me now. Hee-hee!

Scott's entire face goes numb, his heart rate increases and numerous small beads of freezing cold sweat begin to appear on his forehead. He breathes out, almost as if he's deflating, then vomits straight into the toilet. Violently, uncontrollably. The fact that he'd exhaled so much before the vomiting began is preventing him from breathing. His head is hung over the bowl and he struggles to breathe between involuntary muscular spasms, and then collapses onto the floor gasping for breath once the entire contents of his stomach have emptied into the toilet.

*

Julie takes a sip of her gin and tonic and smiles to herself. She's remembering the last time she went out with Scott and his previous overly long toilet jaunt, and wonders if he's managed to be even more lightweight this time. As she sees him coming out of the toilet cubicle, her smile becomes a giggle. It would appear from looking at him that she's right.

*

Jonathan clocks Scott straight away and instantly begins to panic, before recognising that he's strung out on coke. He sees him greet Julie and sit down. He can't afford for them to see him. He doesn't let Riz know his concerns at this stage. He decides it's for the best if he gets the drinks and sits quietly in a corner unnoticed, rather than doing anything hasty that could attract their attention.

*

"I wonder if you can help me. I'm looking for Julie Newton," Jerry says to the officer manning the desk at Holme Bridge police station.

"Julie who?"

"Julie Newton, she works for the *Gazette*. I believe she was with one of your officers at the incident on the Cherry Tree Estate this afternoon."

"And who do I say is looking for her?"

Jerry tries to think of a simple believable lie. It comes to him.

"I'm her photographer."

The police officer scans him up and down. "Where's your camera?"

Fucking brilliant, thinks Jerry, I've found the only competent copper in fucking town. "It's in the car. I need to ask her what photographs she wants, boss wants them on his desk by five."

*

Back in the bar, Julie can sense something's not right. "Scott, are you sure you're ok? You look a bit peaky," she asks, suspicious.

"Oh, I'm fucking fine, love. Just, you know, relieved like. Well, pleased in fact. We've done it. We've got the fucking cunt." Scott fidgets as he's speaking and sweat is pouring off him. Julie has her suspicions about what he was up to in the toilet but doesn't want to believe it of him and, if she's honest with herself, she doesn't really have him down as the drug-taking type.

At the far opposite corner of the pub, Rizwan takes a swig of his J20. "You're right. I think it is them. Picture wasn't that good on the news, though."

"I was there, remember? It's definitely them, I know it. The same pair who were coming to see me in the hospital. No question."

"Funny…"

"What is?"

"That's the same fucking copper that nicked me for drink-driving when you grassed me up all those years ago. Look at him, the hypocrite. He looks off his fucking tits."

"I know. I'm considering going to the bog to see if he's left any coke in there."

"Hee-hee, I thought you were a changed man now?"

"Yeah, I am, but… you know. One step at a fucking time. Rome wasn't built in a day, and all that… Nah, fuck it, I'll put it out of my head. I'll go for a fag though, I'll be back in a bit."

"I think you're best staying here, mate. We need to wait until they've gone. If you go hopping about on those crutches, you'll attract attention. You're lucky they were distracted when we came in."

"I suppose. But we don't really have time."

"The only thing you don't really have is a choice, mate. We'll just sit tight. By the look of him, it won't be long until they leave anyway."

Scott downs his drink, then takes a swipe at his mouth with the back of his hand looking like a vampire that's tasted first blood. "Get to the bar then, Jules."

"Jules? When have you ever called me Jules?"

"What?"

The voice in Scott's head begins to realise that his grasp of control may not be quite as tight as he'd thought. Julie also realises that something is seriously wrong, and quickly has to face up to the reality that she's been let down by a local police officer once again. As fast as she realises this, Scott takes control of his mind.

"Julie, please help me."

"Scott, you're freaking me out. What's wrong?"

"I don't know. I'm sorry, I can't understand it. Can we go, please? Somewhere where we can talk. I'll try to explain."

Julie stares at him and notices that his face has changed. His eyes look different now, more relaxed. Is whatever he's taken wearing off, she wonders, or is there something bigger going on? She can see a sincerity and an honesty in him, but he seems confused. She decides to give him one more chance.

*

Jerry rounds the corner from the police station, spots the Dog and Duck at the end of the street, dips his head to shield it from the rain and continues towards the entrance. He's unsure of what to do. Will he wait in the freezing cold, or just go in there? What if they've gone somewhere else? All bridges he'll cross as and when he gets to them.

*

Inside, Julie is once again having to help Scott out of a pub, walking with her arm around his waist and his around her shoulder. His eyes are rolling. She doesn't know whether she should be taking him home or to a hospital, but opts for taking him home as it's nearer, just around the corner. Perhaps she can bring him round before an ambulance is needed. After all, if this is drug-related, he'll get fired if he ends up being found out.

"Look, they're going," says Rizwan

"Thank fuck for that. Look at the state of him, too. He's a fucking mess."

As Jonathan finishes his sentence, Scott and Julie have just left the pub. He and Rizwan turn their attention towards the window and watch them. Or, more specifically, Julie struggling to hold Scott up as they're blown and blasted around by the weather. Then they see something neither of them was expecting.

"Would you like a hand?" asks Jerry, approaching them and lifting Scott's free arm over his shoulder.

"Erm, thanks," says Julie. She kind of recognises him but she can't put her finger on where from.

"What's wrong with him?" Jerry asks, looking across and down and the limp body he's helping her drag along.

"I don't know. I just need to get him home. He only lives

round the corner." .

Rizwan reaches into his jacket pocket, pulls out a mobile phone, passes it to Jonathan and says, "Keep hold of this. I'll see where they're going and then I'll give you a ring."

"I'll come with you."

"No you won't, you'll slow me down and attract too much attention, hobbling along on those crutches. Just sit tight and wait here."

Rizwan doesn't wait for a response, he just leaves his drink and heads off out to follow them. He can feel his heart pounding in his chest and he's unsure of what's going on, or what he should do. There's no telling what Jerry could have done but then there was always a chance that the police had it wrong. However, if they did have it wrong, what was Jerry doing helping the copper? None of it makes any sense to him.

They round the corner onto Common Street, and continue along until they reach Scott's house at number 16. Rizwan is too far away to see the number on the door, but counts down how many houses away it is from him and then turns around and heads back to the pub to get Jonathan.

Jerry props Scott up whilst Julie goes rummaging through his jacket to look for the keys. As he stands there, he ponders the situation he's in briefly and realises that he needs to immobilise Julie as soon as possible. He knows he can't hang around once they've gone inside as it'd look suspicious, and Scott won't cause him a problem; he can barely stand. As she opens the door, Jerry carefully carries Scott inside, follows her through to the living room and plonks him on the sofa. Then he scans the room and casually flips up his wrist. The bat concealed in his sleeve falls out and he catches it by the handle, then follows Julie into the kitchen.

*

Rizwan bursts through the doors of the pub gasping for breath and shouts out at Jonathan to come with him. Jonathan struggles to his feet with the crutches and swings his way towards the exit to join Rizwan.

"I thought you were going to ring me," he complains as he approaches.

"Payphone's smashed," explains Rizwan, gasping for breath. "They're only around the corner."

*

Jerry looks down at Julie, who is stunned from the full force smack he just gave her to the side of the neck. He'd heard that if you struck someone on the side of the neck, you were pretty much guaranteed a knockout. Not in Julie's case, though. He cracked her but, in the split second before the impact, he wavered, having a brief moment of worry about whether he'd break her neck or not, the result being that he ended up not hitting her hard enough.

She's stunned though, kind of rolling around and wobbling like a fly that's been swatted and survived. Jerry turns his attention towards Scott, who's now fitting on the sofa. Jerry grabs him and as he lifts him forward, Scott vomits all over himself. Jerry knows he needs to act fast and secure the two of them so that he can buy some time while he thinks of what to do. He has flashbacks of searching through the kitchen all those years ago when he was in a similar situation with his Uncle Jack. He heads towards it; there's always something that can be found in a kitchen to tie people up with.

*

Rizwan tries hard to cover up his frustration at having to keep slowing down for Jonathan, but the look on his face every time he has to stop and wait for him to catch up is a giveaway.

"I'm sorry, Riz, I'm moving as fast as I can."

"I know, mate, I know. It's alright, I'm sorry I'm just worried, that's all. Do you want a hand?"

"No, I'll be fine. Come on!"

*

Julie tries to let out a scream but the sock shoved into her mouth muffles it. As Jerry brings the hammer down on the nail in her foot, she screams in agony again. Why tie them up, he thought, when he can just nail them to these nice looking floorboards?

Scott was passed out on the couch, and although it had been difficult keeping Julie still at the beginning of the process, now that both her hands and her left foot were pinned to the floor, she seemed to have stopped trying to wriggle free. It's hardly surprising, he figured. It must be painful as hell to try and move if you're nailed to something.

*

As they approach the house, they pause. Neither of them has thought it through carefully enough. They know they can't just go barging in. What if Jerry didn't know anything and was simply being helpful? He might not even still be in there.

Rizwan grabs control of the situation.

"Right," he says, "you just stay here and keep a look-out. I'm going to head into the back garden and see what I can see through the windows. I'll be back in a bit."

"Well, just be careful, yeah?"

"Yeah. If I'm not back in five minutes you'll have to call the police. Use that mobile I gave you. See you in a bit."

Riz heads through the front gate, into the garden and carefully creeps towards the living room window. He peers inside to see Jerry dragging Scott across the living room floor and into the kitchen. From where he is, he can see Julie's body lying on the floor in the kitchen but he can't make out the reason why she's immobile. Quietly and carefully, he leaves the garden and heads back to Jonathan.

"Right. He's definitely up to something but whatever he's doing, he's doing it in the kitchen. I'm going to go round the back and see if I can get a better look."

"Look, are you sure this is a good idea? I mean, there's no need to get hurt, we can just walk away now."

"Listen, I know what you're saying, but it could be something completely innocent. I can't believe that Jerry would be involved in something illegal. After all, the copper was pretty much flaked out when they left the boozer, in which case Jerry might not even know how close he is to being in bother. The flipside is that if I'm wrong, and he has done something and targeted them, then they'll need our help."

*

The first nail busts through the soft flesh on the underside of Scott's hand and cracks the bone as it powers through to the floorboards. His previously sleepy eyes widen and the pupils shrink as the shock brings him straight back into consciousness. He swings out with his free arm, making contact with the side of Jerry's head, but Jerry's so focused on what he's doing that he barely flinches. He strikes the nail again, securing Scott's hand to the kitchen floor. Scott tried to strike out again but Jerry catches his hand and thrusts it towards the floor, then whips another large nail from his pocket and attempts to hammer it in. Unfortunately for Jerry, though, Scott isn't having any of it and won't keep his hand still for long enough for Jerry to get the nail in. Jerry shifts his attentions and decides to concentrate on knocking Scott back out so he can finish securing him. He sits on Scott's chest and he grasps his throat tightly. Scott waves his free arm, manically swiping left to right at Jerry's arms to release the grip, but it's no good. Jerry pulls his right arm away from the throat and punches Scott in the face hard and rapidly.

He continues to punch until Scott's free arm stops waving around and flops to the floor. Then he calmly pauses to catch his breath for a few seconds before continuing with the hammer and nails.

Rizwan sees it all through the window. He's so stunned with the horror of what he is witnessing that he's frozen to the spot, sick to the stomach, unable to move until suddenly he notices a movement. Julie has raised her head and is looking directly at him, desperate pleading in her eyes.

Shocked out of his trance, he ducks away and scurries back to the front of the house and out of the gate. Once on the main road, he collapses on the floor in a shock, thinking he's about to be sick.

"What the fuck's wrong with you? You look like you've seen a ghost," says Jonathan.

"We need to call the police. We need to call them now. I think he's going to kill them." Rizwan's voice is a feeble croak.

"No, Riz, I told you no police. If they turn up, they'll arrest me for sure. I can't risk it. And without Jerry, I've got nowhere else to go!"

"So you're saying you'd rather let him kill them? Is that what you're saying?"

"What do you mean, 'kill them'? You mean Jerry? What are

you talking about? What have you seen?"

Rizwan tells him and now it's Jonathan's turn to go pale and feel sick.

"Jerry's our friend," he says feebly. "What if we go in there and talk him out of it? The copper will have to let me go then, if I've saved his life."

"I don't know, mate, he's fucking manic. You should see Jerry, he's lost it. You know how big he is. There's no way I'd consider taking him on in a fight if he was in a good mood, never mind like he was in there, man."

"Look, we've got the element of surprise on our side. I'm not saying we should jump him or anything, but the shock of seeing us should knock him sideways a bit. He'll listen to us, surely? We should be able to talk some sense into him."

Rizwan pulls himself to his feet as he ponders Jonathan's plan. "I think we need a side plan."

"A side plan?"

"Yeah, a back-up."

"Like what?"

"Like the police."

"I've fucking told you –"

"No, let me finish. We'll write out a text on the phone but not send it. Put the address on and say who's in the house. If this is that copper's house, they'll be round here in a flash. We should type it now so that if something goes wrong, it just needs sending. Then we have a back-up."

Jonathan expels air in a massive sigh before agreeing that as a back-up plan, it's acceptable.

*

Inside the house, Jerry has secured Scott and pulled himself up a chair between the two of them. He's not sat down on it yet, though. Deciding that he could now do with Scott awake, he's stood above him, pissing all over his face.

Julie is trying to scream at him to stop but it's going unnoticed. He finishes and zips himself away, then turns to Julie. "I'll be getting that out again later for you." He grins and licks his lips as he contemplates the pleasures to come.

Then he stands over Scott again and lightly kicks him in the side of the head. After a couple of taps, Scott comes around again. His first reaction is to try and speak but the sock in his mouth prevents it.

"Well, here we are then," says Jerry, pacing around the two of them. "The fucking slag and the copper."

He kneels down in front of Julie, rips open her top and sqeezes her breasts hard. "Do you remember me now, Julie?" he asks her.

She screams and her eyes fill up, but Jerry shows no remorse. "Is that a no? Do you want me to jog your memory?" He slides his hand up her skirt and along the inside of her thigh.

Julie's instant reaction is to try and close her legs but the nails in her feet prevent it and as she tries to move, shooting pains fire straight up both of her legs. He continues up the skirt, then moves his hand into her underwear and forces his finger inside her. "Remember now?"

Then he pulls away from her and moves his attention to Scott. "And you! You fucking miserable, slimy fuck! You think I don't know you from Adam, I bet. I know exactly who you are, Scott Dempsey. Exactly, and do you want to know the worst thing? Well, worst for me, not for you. The worst thing was that you nearly got away without being killed. I was going to let you off! Both of you, actually. I'd hung up my hat until you killed my fucking guinea pig, you wankers.

"So now you're both here and you're going to die just as I'd intended all along. And why? Well, it'd only be right to tell you,

I suppose. Julie, you made my life a living hell through school. I was constantly mocked and had the piss taken out of me and all because you refused to admit what we'd done. Well, I hope you're fucking pleased with yourself now. And you, Dempsey, you horrible little cunt! You fucked my sister off once she'd gotten pregnant. Just left her. She told me who you were and, to be honest, you've been my most ambitious and interesting project of all. My programme of torture for you didn't involve toxins or blades, just some very carefully placed posters and pictures, nothing special. Just triggers, just enough for you to notice them on an unconscious level, rather than a conscious one."

Jerry reaches into his pocket and pulls out a picture. It's a shot of the head and shoulders of a woman. Scott's dream woman. "Recognise her, do you? Hee-hee.. If all the work I put in had gone as it was intended to, you should have been dreaming about her for – ooh, I don't know… About twelve or eighteen fucking months or so.

"I suppose you're curious to know who she is, too. Well, once my sister confessed to me that her husband wasn't my nephew's father and that the real dad wanted nothing to do with her. I took your name and started to do a little bit of digging. You see, not wanting kids must be hereditary, because it turns out that you were adopted. Your mum didn't want you. How do you feel about that? You may or may not have known it, but that's by the by. The fact is, you had a sister, two years younger than you, so I tracked her down. Took this picture of her. She's pretty, isn't she, don't you think?"

Scott can't understand. All this was explained away in the counselling, it all made sense. He remembers a very brief relationship with a girl who had told him she was pregnant, but he'd just assumed it was bullshit, designed to trap him. The voice in his head is struggling to understand, too and internally, Scott begins to argue with himself over whose fault it is he's in this situation.

*

Rizwan and Jonathan are still on the doorstep, arguing in whispers over the best course of action to take once they're in there. They were waiting until Jerry finished talking. They could hear the mumbles through the door and knew that whilst he was talking to them, he couldn't be doing much else to them. It makes more sense to go in calmly, rather than barge in and confuse or irritate him.

Rizwan grabs the door handle and pushes it down slowly, then steps through the front door and into the living room, with Jonathan lurching behind him on his crutches.

Hearing them enter, Jerry turns his head. "Rizwan! What the fuck are you doing here? And Tarquin! I thought you were fucking dead."

"Listen, it's a long story, mate, but what the fuck are you doing?" Jonathan says.

"We came to see if we can talk you out of here. You don't want to hurt these two," adds Rizwan.

"Riz, I suggest you and faggot boy here better just turn around, fuck off out and forget you ever came here." Jerry's voice is cold and flat.

"No, Jerry, we won't."

Jonathan is impressed at Rizwan's resolve but Jerry's whole demeanour is terrifying. He still looks like Jerry but the eyes are different. They seem wider, his head is dipped as if he has to look upwards to see straight, and his breathing is slow and deep. Could he be on something? He decides it's for the best to let Riz deal with this. Jerry's memories of Tarquin, as he was formerly nicknamed in the good old days of the Nobody Inn, clearly aren't good ones.

"Listen, Rizwan, just turn around and walk," he urges. "It's for the best."

Rizwan takes no notice, just continues negotiating with Jerry.

*

The voice in Scott's head takes control of his situation. Scott turns his head to glance at Julie, tries to smile as best he can with the cloth in his mouth, then tenses his stomach muscles in an effort to quash the pain as he begins slowly lifting his right hand to try and prise it off the floorboards. Unfortunately, the nail was hammered in so hard that instead of his hand lifting the nail from the floor, the head of the nail begins to sink into the flesh of palm of his hand and he feels the iron spike jarring against his bone.

He tenses up again and tries to clench a fist. This time, despite the pain, he feels the nail give way to the wood a little. Quietly and carefully, he twists and pulls and clenches and relaxes and, in excruciating agony, he slowly but surely pries it away from the wood, all the while using all his control not to make a sound or alert Jerry's attention, and then, with one huge swoop, his bloodied hand lifts from the floor. Scott spots his target, and strikes.

"Aaaaah!" Jerry has turned his attention back to Scott too late to stop the long, sharp nail piercing deep into his calf muscle.

He falls to his knees and, quick as a flash, Scott swings at Jerry again. This time he aims for the temple but falls short, skewering the nail into his cheek. This was a bad move as he has failed to immobilise Jerry who, in one fluid movement, crashes down on top of Scott's chest again and forces his free arm to the floor.

As Scott struggles and writhes in absolute agony, Jerry whips out the hammer from his jacket pocket and begins pounding

Scott's hand furiously. He isn't using the nail to secure Scott's hand to the floor this time, he's simply pounding it, pulverising it, shattering flesh and bone.

*

From the doorway, Jonathan hears a faint, strangled sound – it's Julie, trying to scream. He glances towards Rizwan and quickly realises he's useless in this situation as he's frozen with shock, standing there like a zombie with his jaw hanging open. Julie's eyes find his and he sees the longing and desperation in them, but what can he do? If only he weren't on these fucking crutches!

He swings his eyes back to the centre of the room and sees that Jerry has now brought the hammer up above his head, ready to bring it down onto Scott's. It's now or never. Someone has to do something and even though he's a cripple, that someone has to be him.

Jonathan moves as quickly as he can. Three or four swings with the crutches and he's barged past Rizwan and is in front of Jerry and Scott. Jerry turns his head to look at him and that's his fatal mistake. Jonathan times it just right and catches Jerry in the throat with the butt of his right crutch.

Gasping and gurgling, Jerry rolls off Scott's chest and lands between him and Julie. Jonathan seizes his chance. Quickly, carefully, he swings over the top of Scott and thrusts out his left crutch. Balancing himself on Jerry's Adam's apple, he pushes down with all his weight. Suddenly, there's a loud crack and the crutch gives. With a start, he pulls it back to regain his balance and falls across Jerry and the crutches go flying across the room. That's when he realises it wasn't the crutch that had snapped, it was something in Jerry's neck. He's lying still. Dead? He hopes so. Yet does he? That would mean he'd have two deaths to answer for. A double life sentence. Oh Jesus, oh fuck!

Sickened, he looks to his left, at Scott who's struggling to speak, and pulls the sock from his mouth. "Call the fucking station now!" Scott barks.

Jonathan looks at him nailed there, helpless and can see the agony in his face. "I can't mate. I'm sorry," he says.

"Jonathan, please call them. Now!"

Jerry's not dead. He begins to gurgle and spasm underneath him. Without his crutches, he can't move. His limbs seem to have lost what little strength they had. He turns his head. On his right, Julie, with dried blood in her hair and on her face, is still giving him the same look of intense need. He notices that pools of blood have formed around her feet. He should try to free her... He should... But what if... ?

"Police. Now. It's urgent." While he dithered, Rizwan has taken control and done as Scott wanted.

"No, Riz. Please!" sobs Jonathan. "I can't go to prison. I can't go."

Scott raises his smashed-up hand which is pouring blood, and rests his mangled fingers on Jonathan's shoulder.

"It'll be okay. I promise."

*

Jerry opens his eyes to see his lifeless body beneath him with Jonathan draped across the top of it. He is somewhere up near the ceiling and he looks down at the devastation he's caused, Julie and Scott nailed to the floor and a petrified-looking Rizwan struggling to speak as he phones the police. As he drifts up and away, he spins around to see an almost blinding light. Without hesitation, he reaches out in front of him, then pushes his arms down to his sides to propel himself forwards. The intense light pulsates and vibrates as he gets closer. Almost there, he closes his eyes and covers them to protect them. Now he can see nothing but the burning red of his eyelids and then, after a while, darkness.

He opens his eyes once more and as they begin to adjust, he sees a stunningly beautiful and familiar looking woman. He rubs his eyes in an effort to refocus and, as he blinks, tears roll down his cheeks and with each one, the clarity of his vision becomes clearer and clearer. He turns and looks in the other direction and sees another stunning woman. After a few seconds, he realises that they're all around him. He's surrounded by them. He smiles and glows inwardly, feeling extremely pleased with himself. All along, he'd known deep down that killing all those people who'd so richly deserved it was a good thing. Just as he's about to thank God for his heaven, his smug, euphoric feeling drains away as he realises this isn't heaven after all. He's in a cinema... and the film's about to roll.

PaperBooks

This book has been published by vibrant publishing company Paperbooks. If you enjoyed reading it then you can help make it a major hit. Just follow these three easy steps:

1. Recommend it
Pass it onto a friend to spread word-of-mouth or, if now you've got your hands on this copy you don't want to let it go, just tell your friend to buy their own or maybe get it for them as a gift. Copies are available with special deals and discounts from our own website and from all good bookshops and online outlets.

2. Review it
It's never been easier to write an online review of a book you love and can be done on Amazon, Waterstones.com, WHSmith.co.uk and many more. You could also talk about it or link to it on your own blog or social networking site.

3. Read another of our great titles
We've got a wide range of diverse modern fiction and it's all waiting to be read by fresh-thinking readers like you! Come to us direct at www.legendpress.co.uk to take advantage of our superb discounts. (Plus, if you email info@legend-paperbooks.co.uk just after placing your order and quote 'WORD OF MOUTH', we will send another book with your order absolutely free!)

Thank you for being part of our word of mouth campaign.

info@legend-paperbooks.co.uk
www.paperbooks.co.uk